P9-DGX-610

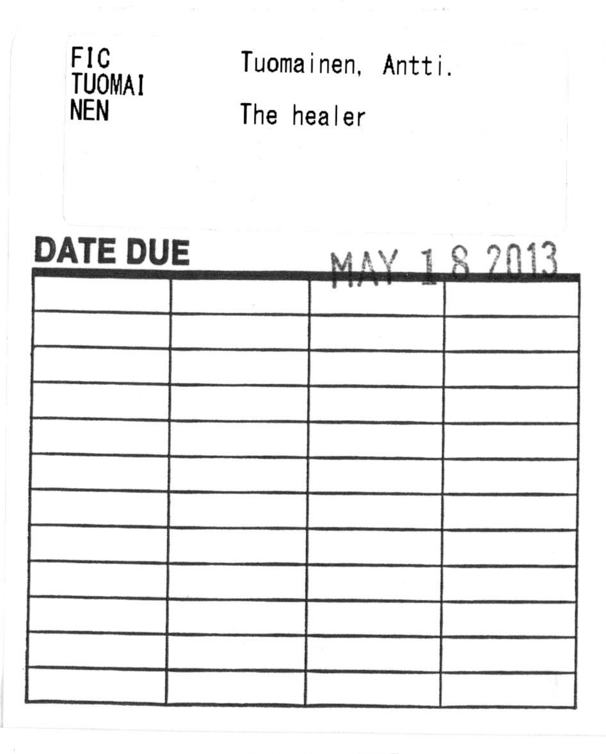
FIC
TUOMAI
NEN
Tuomainen, Antti.
The healer
DATE DUE
MAY 18 2013

THE HEALER

THE HEALER

ANTTI TUOMAINEN

Translated from the Finnish by

LOLA ROGERS

Henry Holt and Company
New York

Henry Holt and Company, LLC
Publishers since 1866
175 Fifth Avenue
New York, New York 10010
www.henryholt.com

Henry Holt® and ® are registered trademarks of
Henry Holt and Company, LLC.

Distributed in Canada by Raincoast Book Distribution Limited

Originally published in Finland in 2010 under the title
Parantaja by Helsinki-Kirirat, Helsinki

Library of Congress Cataloging-in-Publication Data

Tuomainen, Antti.
[Parantaja. English]
The healer/Antti Tuomainen ; translated from the Finnish
by Lola Rogers.—1st ed.
p. cm.
ISBN 978-0-8050-9554-8
1. Disasters—Finland—Fiction. 2. Missing persons—Fiction.
3. Poets, Finnish—Fiction. 4. Helsinki (Finland)—Fiction.
I. Rogers, Lola. II. Title.
PH356.T85P3713 2013
894'.54134—dc23 2012027372

Henry Holt books are available for special promotions and premiums.
For details contact: Director, Special Markets.

First Edition 2013

Designed by Meryl Sussman Levavi

Printed in the United States of America

1 2 3 4 5 6 7 8 9 10

For Anu

THE HEALER

TWO DAYS BEFORE CHRISTMAS

1

WHICH WAS WORSE—COMPLETE CERTAINTY THAT THE WORST HAD happened, or this fear, building up moment by moment? Sudden collapse, or slow, crumbling disintegration?

I lurched with the force of a swerve that shook me out of my wandering thoughts, and looked up.

Yellow-black flames from a wrecked truck lashed the pillar of the pedestrian bridge at the Sörnäinen shore road. The truck looked broken in the middle, embracing the pillar like a pleading lover. Not one of the passing cars slowed down, let alone stopped. They moved to the outside lane as they flew by, passing the burning wreck at the greatest possible distance.

So did the bus I was sitting in.

I opened my rain-soaked parka, found a packet of tissues in the inside pocket, pulled one loose with numb fingers, and dried my face and hair with it. The tissue was drenched through in a moment. I squeezed it into a ball and shoved it into my pocket. I shook drops of water from the hem of my jacket into the space between my knees and the wall, then took my phone out of the pocket of my jeans. I tried to call Johanna again.

The number was still unavailable.

The metro tunnel was closed from Sörnäinen to Keilaniemi because of flooding. The train had taken me as far as Kalasatama, where I'd had to wait for the bus for twenty minutes under a sky pouring rain.

The burning truck was left behind as I went back to watching the news on the screen attached to the back of the driver's bulletproof glass compartment. The southern regions of Spain and Italy had officially been left to their own devices. Bangladesh, sinking into the sea, had erupted in a plague that threatened to spread to the rest of Asia. The dispute between India and China over Himalayan water supplies was driving the two countries to war. Mexican drug cartels had responded to the closing of the U.S.-Mexico border with missile strikes on Los Angeles and San Diego. The forest fires in the Amazon had not been extinguished even by blasting new river channels to surround the fires.

Ongoing wars or armed conflicts in the European Union: thirteen, mostly in border areas.

Estimated number of climate refugees planet-wide: 650–800 million people.

Pandemic warnings: H3N3, malaria, tuberculosis, Ebola, plague.

Light piece at the end: the recently chosen Miss Finland believed that everything would be much better in the spring.

I turned my gaze back to the rain that had been falling for months, a continuous flow of water that had started in September and paused only momentarily since. At least five seaside neighborhoods—Jätkäsaari, Kalasatama, Ruoholahti, Herttoniemenranta, and Marjaniemi—had been continuously flooded, and many residents had finally given up and abandoned their homes.

Their apartments didn't stay empty for long. Even damp, moldy, and partially underwater, they were good enough for the hundreds of thousands of refugees arriving in the country. In the evenings large, bright cooking fires and campfires shone from flooded neighborhoods without power.

I got off the bus at the railway station. It would have been quicker to walk through Kaisaniemi Park, but I decided to go around it, along Kaivokatu. There weren't enough police to monitor both the streets and the parks. Walking through the masses of people around the railway station was something always to be avoided. Panicked people were leaving the city and filling jam-packed trains headed north, with all their possessions in their backpacks and suitcases.

Motionless forms lay curled up in sleeping bags under plastic shelters in front of the station. It was impossible to tell whether they were on their way somewhere or simply lived there. The dazzling glow of tall floodlights mixed at eye level with the shimmer of exhaust fumes, the streetlights, and the garish red, blue, and green of lighted advertisements.

The half-burned central post office stood across from the station, a gray-black skeleton. As I passed it, I tried to call Johanna again.

I reached the Sanomatalo building, stood in line for fifteen minutes waiting to go through security, took off my coat, shoes, and belt, put them back on, and walked to the reception desk.

I asked the receptionist to ring Johanna's boss, who for some reason wasn't answering my calls. I had met him a few times, and my guess was that if the call came from within the building he would answer, and when he learned who it was, he'd let me tell him why I had come.

The receptionist was an icy-eyed woman in her thirties

who, judging by her short hair and controlled gestures, was a former soldier who now guarded the physical integrity of the country's last newspaper, her gun still at her side.

She looked me in the eye as she spoke into the air.

"A man named Tapani Lehtinen . . . I checked his ID. . . . Yes . . . One moment."

She nodded to me, the movement of her head like the blow of an ax.

"What is your business?"

"I'm unable to reach my wife, Johanna Lehtinen."

2

HALF BY MISTAKE, I HAD RECORDED THE LAST PHONE CONVERSATION I'd had with Johanna, and I knew it by heart:

"I'm going to be working late today," she began.

"How late is late?"

"Overnight, probably."

"Inside or outside work?"

"I'm already outside. I have a photographer with me. Don't worry. We're going to talk to some people. We'll keep to public places."

A murmuring sound, the noise of cars, a murmur, a low rumble, and the murmur again.

"Are you still there?" she asked.

"Where would I have gone? I'm at my desk."

A pause.

"I'm proud of you," Johanna said. "The way you keep going."

"So do you," I said.

"I guess so," she said, suddenly quiet, almost whispering.

"I love you. Come home in one piece."

"Sure," she whispered, and her words came quickly now, almost a single chain. "See you tomorrow at the latest. I love you."

A murmur. A crackle. A soft click. Silence.

3

MANAGING EDITOR LASSI UUTELA'S ROUGHLY FORTY-YEAR-OLD FACE was covered in blue-gray stubble, and his eyes showed an irritation that he lacked the ability, and perhaps even the desire, to hide.

He was standing directly in front of me when the elevator doors opened on the fifth floor. He wore a black dress shirt and a thin gray sweater, dark jeans, and sneakers. His arms were crossed over his chest, a position they relinquished with elaborate reluctance as I stepped toward him.

Lassi Uutela's least appealing characteristics—his envy of more accomplished journalists, his tendency to avoid confrontation, his habit of holding grudges, his need to always be right—were all familiar to me from what Johanna had told me. Johanna's and Lassi's views of the job of a reporter and the direction of the paper had been clashing more and more often. The ripples from these clashes had come ashore even at home.

We shook hands for a long time and introduced ourselves even though we knew who we were. For a fleeting moment it felt like I was performing in a bad play. As soon as he got his hand free, Lassi turned and brushed the door open with his fingertips. I followed him as he kicked his feet angrily in front of him, as if dissatisfied with their progress. We arrived at the end of a long hallway where there was a corner office a few meters square.

Lassi sat down at his desk in a black high-backed chair and gestured toward the room's only other chair, a sort of white plastic cup.

"I thought Johanna was working at home today," he said.

I shook my head.

"To tell you the truth, I was hoping to find her here."

Now it was his turn to shake his head. The gesture was impatient and brief.

"The last time I saw Johanna was at yesterday's all-staff meeting, around six o'clock. We went through the jobs in progress as usual, then everybody went their separate ways."

"I spoke with Johanna yesterday evening at about nine o'clock."

"Where was she?" he asked indifferently.

"Outside somewhere," I said, and then, after a pause, more quietly, "I didn't think to ask where."

"So you haven't heard from her for a whole day?"

I shook my head, watching him. His posture, leaning backward, the expression on his face, and the pauses deployed between his words revealed what he was really thinking—that I was wasting his time.

"What?" I asked, as if I didn't understand his body language.

"I was just wondering," he said, "whether this has ever happened before."

"No. Why?"

He puckered up his lower lip and lifted his eyebrows—it looked like each one weighed a ton—and acted as if he expected a reward for raising them.

"No reason. It's just that these days . . . all kinds of things can happen."

"Not to us," I said. "It's a long story, but these things don't happen to us."

"Of course not," Lassi said, in a tone somewhat lacking in conviction. He didn't even bother looking me in the eye. "Of course not."

"What story was she working on?"

He didn't answer right away, just weighed his pen in his hand, perhaps weighing something in his mind as well.

"What was it about?" I pressed, seeing that he wasn't going to begin on his own.

"It's probably stupid of me to share this information with you, but then it was a stupid article," he said, leaning his elbows on the desk and looking at me obliquely, as if to gauge my reaction.

"I understand," I said, and waited.

"It's about the Healer."

I may have flinched. Johanna had told me about the Healer.

She'd got her first e-mail from him right after the family in Tapiola was murdered. Someone who called himself the Healer had taken responsibility for the crime. He said he did it on behalf of ordinary people, to avenge them, and said he was the last voice of truth in a world headed toward destruction—a healer for a sick planet. That's why he had murdered the CEO of a manufacturing company and his family. And that's why he would continue to murder whoever he claimed had contributed to the acceleration of climate change. Johanna had notified the police. They investigated and did what they could. There were now nine executives and politicians who'd been killed altogether, along with their families.

I sighed. Lassi shrugged and looked satisfied with my reaction.

"I told her it wouldn't lead anywhere," he said, and I couldn't help noticing a slightly triumphant tone in his voice. "I told her she wouldn't find out any more than the police had. And our rapidly shrinking readership doesn't want to read about it. It's just depressing. They already know that everything's going to hell in a handbasket."

I looked out into the rain-soaked darkness over Töölö Bay. I knew there were buildings out there, but I couldn't see them.

"Did Johanna already write the article?" I asked when we'd had sufficient time to listen to ourselves and the building breathing.

Lassi leaned back in his chair, put his head against the headrest, and looked at me through half-opened eyes, as if I were not on the other side of his narrow desk but far off on the horizon.

"Why do you ask?" he said.

"Johanna and I always keep in touch with each other," I explained. It occurred to me that when we repeat things, it isn't always for the purpose of convincing other people. "I don't mean constantly. But if nothing else we at least send each other a text message or an e-mail every few hours. Even if we don't really have anything to tell each other. It's usually just a couple of words. Something funny, or sometimes something a little affectionate. It's a habit with us."

This last sentence was purposely emphatic. Lassi listened to me, his face expressionless.

"Now I haven't heard from her for twenty-four hours," I continued, and realized I was directing my words to my own reflection in the window. "This is the longest time in all the ten years we've been together that we haven't been in touch with each other."

I waited another moment before I said something just like all the clichés, not caring a bit how it sounded.

"I'm sure that something has happened to her."

"Something has happened to her?" he said, then paused for several seconds in a way that was becoming familiar. There could be only one purpose for these pauses: to undercut me, to make what I said sound stupid and pointless.

"Yes," I said drily.

Lassi didn't say anything for a moment. Then he leaned forward, paused, and said, "Let's assume you're right. What do you intend to do?"

I didn't have to pretend to think about it. I immediately replied, "There's no point in reporting her disappearance to the police. All they can do is enter it in their records. Disappearance number five thousand twenty-one."

"True," Lassi agreed. "And twenty-four hours isn't a terribly long time, either."

I lifted my arm as if to fend off this statement physically, as well as mentally.

"As I said, we always stay in touch. For us, twenty-four hours *is* a long time."

Lassi didn't need to dig very deep to find his irritation. His voice rose, and at the same time a colder rigidity crept into it, as he quickly said, "We have reporters that are in the field for a week at a time. Then they come back with the story. That's the way it works."

"Has Johanna ever been in the field for a week without contacting you?"

Lassi kept his eyes on me, drummed his fingers on the armrest of his chair, and puckered his lips.

"I admit, she hasn't."

"It's just not like her," I said.

Lassi twisted in his chair and spoke rapidly, as if he wanted to hurry up and make sure he was right: "Tapani, we're trying to put together a newspaper here. There's basically no advertising money, and our rule of thumb is that nobody's interested in anything. Except, of course, sex and porn, and scandals and revelations connected with sex and porn. We sold more papers yesterday than we have in a long time. And I assure you we didn't do it with any in-depth reports about the thousands of missing warheads or investigative articles on how much drinking water we have left. Which, by the way, is about half an hour's worth, from what I can tell. No, our lead story was about a certain singer's bestiality video. That's what the people want. That's what they pay for."

He took a breath and continued in a voice that was even more tense and impatient than before, if that was possible.

"Then I've got reporters, like, for instance, Johanna, who want to tell the people the truth. And I'm always asking them, what fucking truth? And they never have a good answer. All they say is that people should know. And I ask, but do they want to know? And more important, do they want to pay to know?"

When I was sure he had finished, I said, "So you tell them about a no-talent singer and her horse."

He looked at me again, from someplace far away where clueless idiots like me aren't allowed to go.

"We're trying to stay alive."

We sat silently for a moment. Then he opened his mouth again: "Can I ask you something?" he said.

I nodded.

"Do you still write your poetry?"

I expected this. He couldn't resist needling me. The question had the seed of the next question in it. It was meant to indicate that I was on the wrong track when it came to Johanna just like I was when it came to everything else. So what. I decided to give him a chance to continue in the vein he'd chosen. I answered honestly.

"Yes."

"When was the last time you were published?"

Once again, I didn't need to think about my answer.

"Four years ago," I said.

He didn't say anything more, just looked at me with red-rimmed, satisfied eyes like he'd just proven some theory of his to be correct. I didn't want to talk about it anymore. It would have been a waste of time.

"Where does Johanna sit?" I asked.

"Why?"

"I want to see her workstation."

"Normally I wouldn't allow it," Lassi said, looking like his last bit of interest in the whole matter had just evaporated. He glanced nonchalantly past me at the office full of cubicles, which he could see through the glass wall. "But I guess there's not much we do normally anymore, and the office is empty, so go ahead."

I got up and thanked him, but he'd already turned toward his monitor and become absorbed in his typing, as if he'd wished he were someplace else the whole time.

Johanna's workstation was easy to find on the right side of the large, open office. A picture of me led me to it.

Something lurched inside me when I saw the old snapshot and imagined Johanna looking at it. Could she see the same difference in my eyes that I saw?

In spite of the large stacks of paper, her desk was well

organized. Her closed laptop lay in the middle of the table. I sat down and looked around. There were a dozen or more workstations, which the reporters called clovers, in the open office space, with four desks at each station. Johanna's desk was on the window side and had a direct view into Lassi's office. Or rather, the upper section of his office—cardboard was stacked against the lower half of the glass walls. The view from the window wasn't much to look at. The Kiasma art museum with its frequently patched copper roof loomed like a gigantic shipwreck in the rain—black, tattered, run aground.

The top of the desk was cool to the touch but quickly grew damp under my hand. I glanced toward Lassi Uutela's office and then looked around. The place was deserted. I slid Johanna's computer into my bag.

There were dozens of sticky notes on the desk. Some of them simply had a phone number or a name and address; a few were complete notes written in Johanna's precise, delicate hand.

I looked through them one by one. There was one in the most recent batch that caught my attention: "H—West–East/North–South" then two lists of neighborhoods—"Tapiola, Lauttasaari, Kamppi, Kulosaari" and "Tuomarinkylä, Pakila, Kumpula, Kluuvi, Punavuori"—with dates next to them.

"H" must mean the Healer. I shoved the note in my pocket.

Next I went through the piles of papers. Most of them were about pieces Johanna had already written: articles about the alleged closing of Russia's nuclear power plants, the dwindling Finnish tax base, the collapse in food quality.

One pile was entirely about the Healer. It included printed copies of all his e-mails. Johanna had written her own notes on the printouts, so many on some that they nearly obscured the original text. I crammed the whole stack into my bag without reading them, got up, and stood looking at the abandoned desk. It was like any other desk, impersonal and indistinguishable from a million others. Still, I hoped it would tell me something, reveal what had happened. I waited a moment, but the desk was still just a desk.

Twenty-four hours earlier, Johanna had sat here.

And she would still be sitting here, if something hadn't happened to her.

I couldn't explain why I was so sure of it. It was as hard to define as the connection between us. I knew that Johanna would call me, if only she could.

I took a step away from the desk, unable at first to take my eyes off her papers, her handwriting, the little objects on the table. Then I remembered something.

I went back to the door of Lassi Uutela's office. He took no notice of me, so I knocked on the door frame. The plastic cracked against the back of my hand. I was surprised at the loud, hollow sound it made. Lassi stopped his hurriedly typing fingers and left his hands waiting in the air as he turned his head. The irritation in his red-rimmed eyes didn't seem to have diminished.

I asked which photographer had been on the job with Johanna, although I had already guessed who it was.

"Gromov," Lassi growled.

I knew him, of course. I'd even met him. Tall, dark, and handsome. Something of a ladies' man, according to Johanna, obsessive when it came to his work, and apparently in everything else as well. Johanna respected Vasili Gromov's skill at his job and liked working with him. They had spent a lot of time together on jobs in Finland and abroad. If anyone had any information about Johanna, it would be him.

I asked Lassi if he'd seen Gromov. He understood immediately what I meant. He picked up his telephone, leaned his head against the headrest on his chair, and aimed his gaze at the ceiling, either toward the air conditioner duct or toward heaven.

"This world's a fucking mess," he said quietly.

4

As I made my way home, Lassi's questions about why I was still writing poetry rose up in my mind again. I hadn't told him what I was thinking. I didn't want to. Lassi wasn't a person you confided in or trusted any more than you had to. But what would I have said, what reason would I have given, for keeping at something that had no future? I would have told him the truth.

To keep writing was to keep living. And I didn't keep living or writing to find readers. People were trying to survive from one day to the next, and poetry didn't have much to do with it. My reasons for writing were completely selfish.

Writing gave my days a shape, a routine. The words, the sentences, the short lines, brought an order to my life that had disappeared all around me. Writing meant that the fragile thread between yesterday, today, and tomorrow was still unbroken.

I tried to read Johanna's papers, but I couldn't concentrate on anything because of the clatter of beer cans and other trash on the bus. They were thrown there by drunken teenagers who were no real danger to the other passengers, but it was still annoying. The late-night routes were another matter, especially the ones without security guards.

I got off the bus at the Herttoniemi metro station. I gave a wide berth to a gang of drunken skinheads—a dozen bald scalps that shone with rain and tattoos—avoided the persistent panhandlers patrolling in front of the shops, and headed toward home in the dark evening. There was a break in the rain, and the strong, gusting wind couldn't decide which direction to blow. It lunged here and there, grabbing onto everything with its strong hands, including the brightly lit security lights on the walls of the buildings, which made it look as if the houses themselves were swaying in the evening darkness. I walked briskly past the day care that had first been abandoned by children, then scrawled on by random passersby, and finally set on fire. The church at the other side of the intersection had an emergency shelter for the homeless, and it looked like it was full to the brim—the previously bright vestibule was half-dim with people. A few minutes later I turned onto the path to our apartment building.

The roof of the building opposite had been torn off in an autumn storm and still hadn't been repaired, and the top-floor apartments were dark. Soon we would be facing the same thing, like people in a thousand other buildings. They weren't designed for continuous high winds and rain for half the year, and by the time people realized that the wind and rain were here to stay it was too late. Besides, no one had the money or the interest to keep up a building where power and water outages made living unpleasant and probably eventually impossible.

The lock on the street door recognized my card, and the door opened. When the power was out we used the old cut key. Keys like that should have been unnecessary, should have been history, but like many other objects and ideas once considered relics, they managed to do what the newer ones couldn't: they worked.

I tried the lights in the stairwell, but the switch was out of order again. I climbed to the second story in the dark, using the stair railing as a guide, arrived at our door, opened both safety locks and the ordinary lock, turned off the alarm, and, instinctively, breathed in.

The smell of the place had everything in it: morning coffee, a hurried spritz of perfume, the pine soap from washing the rugs the summer before, the long Christmas holidays, the armchair we bought together, every night spent with the person you love. It was all there in that smell, and it was all connected together in my mind, although the place had been aired out a thousand times. The smell was so familiar that I was just about to announce that I was home, automatically. But there was no one there to hear me.

I carried my bag into the kitchen, took out the papers and the laptop, and put them on the table. I warmed up the vegetable casserole Johanna had made over the weekend and sat down to eat. Somewhere a couple of floors up lived some devoted music lovers. The beat was so low, steady, and repetitive that it was easy to believe it would carry on forever—nothing short of massive intervention would ever stop its progress.

Everything I saw on the table and tasted in my mouth and thought in my head confirmed my fear that something bad had happened. An outsized lump rose in my throat and made it difficult to swallow, and I felt a squeezing around my chest and abdomen that suddenly forced me to concentrate entirely on breathing.

I pushed my plate aside and turned on Johanna's computer. The hum of the machine and the glow of the screen filled the kitchen. The very first thing I saw was the desktop image: Johanna and I on our honeymoon ten years ago.

More swallowing.

The two of us in the foreground, younger in many ways, above us an almost palpably blue southern European sky, behind us Florence's Ponte Vecchio, beside us a patch of the uneven, ancient wall of a house and the gilded sign of a riverside café, half illegible from the dazzle of sunlight.

I looked at Johanna's laughing eyes, aimed straight ahead—reflecting green as well as blue in the bright light of April—her slightly wide mouth, her even, white teeth, the very beginnings of tiny wrinkles, and the short, curly hair that bordered her face like spring petals.

I opened the folders on the computer desktop.

In the folder marked "New" I found a subfolder "H." I realized I had guessed correctly: "H" was for Healer. I went through the documents. Most of them were Johanna's text files, some were news videos, links, and articles from other papers. The most recent text file was from yesterday. I clicked it open.

The piece was nearly finished. Johanna would certainly be using most of it in her final article. As soon as she writes it, I reminded myself.

It began with a description of the multiple murder in Tapiola. A family of five had been killed in the early morning hours, and someone using the pseudonym "the Healer" had announced himself as the perpetrator. According to the police investigation, the father of the family was the last to die: the CEO of a large food company and an advocate for the meat processing industry, he'd had to look on, with his hands and feet tied and his mouth taped, as his wife and three small children were each cold-bloodedly executed with a gunshot to the head. He was murdered last, with a single bullet to the center of his forehead.

Johanna had interviewed the police investigator, the interior minister, and a representative of a private security company. The piece ended with an extended plea from Johanna, directed as much at the police and the public as it was at the Healer himself.

I also found a map of Helsinki and a chart Johanna had made of the date and location of each murder, the times she received the e-mails, and the main contents of the messages. This had to do with the sticky note I'd found. I looked at it again: West–East or North–South. The map clearly showed that the murders had progressed chronologically, first from west to east, then from north to south.

Based on Johanna's summaries of the contents of the messages, the e-mails had grown darker as the murders reached the south side of the city. Some of the messages also had a surprisingly personal tone: Johanna was addressed using her first name and praised for her "truthful and uncompromising" journalism. The writer even seemed to believe that she would understand the necessity for this kind of extreme action.

The second-to-last message had come the day after the murders in Punavuori. A family of four—a father who owned and operated a large chain of car dealerships, his wife, and their two sons, aged ten and twelve—were found dead in their home. Without the e-mail message, the deaths would probably have been classified as another of the murder-suicides that were occurring weekly. The suicide theory was supported by the fact that the large-caliber weapon the murders were committed with was found in the father's hand, as if he were handing it to the police as proof.

Then the Healer's message arrived. The address was given in the e-mail—Kapteenikatu 14—with an admonition to investigate the matter more thoroughly.

This was duly done, and it became clear that although the

gun had been in the father's hand, someone else had helped him aim and shoot. So he had felt each shot in his hand and body and seen and heard his own children die from bullets that came from a gun he was holding.

The last message was hastily and poorly written—stilted in both grammar and content. It didn't defend the crimes in any way.

I got up from the table, walked to the balcony, and stood there for a long time. I breathed in the cool air, trying to blow away the invisible stone on my chest. The stone lightened, but it didn't roll away completely.

We'd moved into our place almost immediately after we married. The apartment had become a home and the home had become dear to us; it was our place in the world—a world that was completely different ten years ago. Of course it was easy to say afterward that all the warning signs were already visible then—the summer stretching out long and dry into autumn, rainy winters, increasingly high winds, news about hundreds of millions of people wandering the world, and exotic insects appearing in our own yards, on our own skin, spreading Lyme disease, malaria, sandfly fever, encephalitis.

Our building was on a high hill in Herttoniemi, and on a clear day you could see across the bay from the living room and balcony all the way to Arabianranta, where most of the houses were continuously flooded. Like many other neighborhoods that suffered from flooding, Arabianranta was often dark. They didn't dare let electricity in because of the water that remained in the badly damaged buildings. With the naked eye, from two and a half kilometers away, I could see dozens of fires along the shore. From where I stood they looked small and delicate, like just-lit matches that could easily be blown out. The reality was otherwise. The fires were as much as a meter and a half in diameter. People used all kinds of things they found on the shore and in abandoned buildings as fuel. There were rumors that they used dead animals, even people.

It was strange how I'd got used to seeing the fires. I couldn't have told you when the first ones appeared or when the evening ribbon of flames they formed became a daily sight.

Farther off, beyond the silhouette of the buildings on the shore, were the modern towers of Pasila, and the blaze and glow to the left told me where the city center was. Over it all lay a dark, boundless night sky that held the whole world in its cold, sure grip.

I realized that I was looking for connections between what I'd just read and what I was now seeing.

Johanna.

Out there somewhere.

Like I'd told Lassi, there was no point in my going to the police. If they didn't have the time or the resources to look for the murderer of these families, how would they have the time to look for a woman missing for twenty-four hours, one of thousands of missing people?

The Healer.

West–East or North–South.

The night didn't seem to hold any answers. The music thumped upstairs. The wind moved through the trees on the slope of the ridge below, singing through the bare branches as well as it could but able to prevail against the barrier of human and machine-made sound only for brief moments. The cold of the balcony's cement floor on the soles of my feet prompted me to seek warmth.

I returned to the kitchen table, read through all of Johanna's documents on the Healer one more time, made some coffee, and tried to call her again. It was no surprise when the number could not be reached. It was also no surprise that a hint of panic and desperation was beginning to splash through my worried mind.

There was one thing I could be sure of: Johanna had disappeared on a job investigating something connected with the Healer.

I pushed all other thoughts aside, drank my coffee, and read the printouts of the e-mails the Healer had sent to Johanna, in the order they were received. As I read them, I sorted them into two piles. In the first, I put messages where the necessity of the crimes was defended, sometimes at great length, and Johanna's previous articles were mentioned, sometimes with the implication that her work was something like the Healer's—to uncover lies and to liberate. The other pile contained the messages that directly stated where the murder victims could be found and contained only a few hastily and poorly written lines.

I leafed through the piles again and came to the same conclusion that I had the first time. There were two authors. At least in theory. At least that's what I thought.

I opened the map Johanna had made again. It was like a pocket guide to hell. I moved through the red points marking the murders, went through the dates and Johanna's figures. There were two or three days between the murders. Johanna had added a question mark to each of the four points of the compass and calculated possible locations of future murders.

As I stared at the map, the icon for Johanna's e-mail program caught my eye. I hesitated. Reading another person's e-mail is undoubtedly wrong. But maybe this situation was an exception. Besides, we didn't have any secrets from each other, did we? I decided that I would open her e-mail only if the situation absolutely demanded it. In the meantime I would get by strictly on what related directly to the article Johanna was working on now.

I remembered the phone call I'd recorded, turned on my own laptop, and plugged my phone into it.

I copied the last conversation I'd had with Johanna onto the computer, searched a moment for the right program, downloaded it, and opened the audio file with it. The audio editing software was easy to use. I separated the sounds, removed my and Johanna's voices, and listened. I could hear the noise of cars, a rumble, and the same murmuring sound I'd heard before. I listened to it again and again, then separated out the rumble and the sound of cars until I was able to make out the tone of the murmur by itself. With a hopeful feeling I seemed to hear something regularly repeating, not wind or the brush of coat sleeves but something with a much more even rhythm: waves. I played the file again and shut my eyes, trying to listen and remember at the same time.

Was it the sound of waves, or was I just hearing what I wanted to hear?

I let the sound play in a loop and looked at Johanna's map and calculations. Maybe this murmur, its regular repetition, really did indicate the sea or the seashore. Assuming that the murders occurred over a two- or three-day cycle, then the points set apart by dates and question marks, following the Healer's crimes from north to south—however roughly—would converge somewhere around Jätkäsaari, on the southwest shore of the city.

Furthermore, assuming that Johanna had come to the same conclusion, then that would have been the area she called me from the last time we spoke.

5

The taxi driver, a young North African man, didn't speak Finnish and didn't want to use the meter. That suited me. We agreed on a price, half in English, half using our fingers, and the meter was left glowing four zeros in the dark car as he accelerated away from my apartment and onto Hiihtomäentie, past the metro station and the abandoned shopping center and across the overpass toward Itäväylä. He avoided the potholes and cracks in the road as skillfully as he did drivers who made dangerous passes or swerved out of their lanes.

The waterfront homes at Kulosaari were, with a few exceptions, among the first houses left empty by their owners and were now filled with new arrivals. Those who had the means had moved north: those with the most means to northern Canada, the rest to Finnish, Swedish, and Norwegian Lapland. Dozens of high-security, privately owned small towns had been established in the north in recent years, both on the Arctic coast and in the interior, with self-contained water, sewage, and electrical systems—and, of course, hundreds of uniformed guards to keep out undesirables.

Now the majority of those living in the dark houses of Kulosaari were refugees from the east and south. A string of tents and campfires lined the shore. The coexistence between the refugees and the tenacious original inhabitants defending their houses and shoreline wasn't always peaceful. The Healer would no doubt have had an opinion about that, as well.

As we drove I looked through the news videos in Johanna's H file. The closer they got to the present, the more exasperated the reporters were in their questions, and the more exhausted the police were in their answers. The statements of the red-eyed police inspector in charge of the investigation were, in the end, confined to the comment "We will continue to investigate and let you know when we have any new information." I moved his name from the screen to my phone memory and looked up his number. Chief Inspector Harri Jaatinen.

I leaned back in my seat.

When had I known for certain that something had happened to Johanna? When I woke up at four in the morning and heard a dog barking? Making coffee two hours later, after it became obvious that getting up would be less trouble than continuing to try to go back to sleep? Or did the doubt change to fear over the hours of the day as I mechanically did my work, checking my telephone every other minute?

The young cab driver was good at his job—he knew where the roads were out and proceeded accordingly. When we got to Pitkäsilta we stopped at the intersection and a stretch SUV pulled up beside us with its rear window open. I quickly counted eight young men inside—their expressionless faces, their forward-focused lazy-lidded eyes, and their tattooed necks told me they weren't just gang members but also probably armed. As the SUV pulled into traffic, not one man's expression faltered.

There was a fire in Kaisaniemi Park. Judging by the height of the flames, it must have been a car or something. The massive column of flame was like the mark of a bacchanal in the otherwise lightless night. At the corner of Vilhonkatu and Mikonkatu I heard gunshots and saw three men running toward the park. They disappeared before the echo of the shots had faded. People were kicking a man lying prostrate in front of the Natural History Museum. Then someone, apparently the strongest of the group, started dragging him by his filthy clothes toward the metro tunnel entrance, perhaps planning to throw him down the shaft.

We arrived at Temppeliaukio in twenty minutes. I shoved a bill through the narrow opening in the Plexiglas and got out of the car.

The modern dome of Temppeliaukio Church was gone; what was left of the building resembled ancient stone ruins perched high on a rock. The fragments of wall cast long shadows all the way to Lutherinkatu. Surrounded by the yellowish light of the street lamps, the shadows were black as pitch, as if painted on the ground. Someone had taken a PARKING PROHIBITED sign from its pole and thrown it into the middle of the street. The sign looked like it had finally given up on prohibiting anything.

The night was as cold in Töölö as it had been at home in Herttoniemi, but not as quiet. Cars could be heard here and there, the honk of horns, Finnish rock, people shouting, even people having fun. Above all the noise a woman's bright laugh sounded carefree, and stranger than anything I'd heard in a long time.

Ahti and Elina Kallio were friends of ours—it was Johanna and Elina's friendship that first brought us together. And no, Elina hadn't heard from Johanna.

I stood in the foyer of their apartment, took off my rain-soaked jacket and shoes, and listened to Elina and Ahti ask questions in turn:

"Where do you think she might be?"

"She hasn't called you at all?"

"And no one knows where she is?"

Finally Ahti asked a question that I knew how to answer.

"Yes, I'd like some coffee. Thanks."

Ahti disappeared into the kitchen, and Elina and I went into the living room, where two floor lamps in opposite corners and one calmly fluttering candle on the dark wood table in the middle of the room gave the place a softer light than was perhaps desirable. Somehow I felt that at that moment I needed a different atmosphere, more light, something decisively brighter.

I sat on the sofa. Elina was in the armchair across from me. She pulled a light brown wool shawl onto her lap, not spreading it out but not leaving it folded, either. It sat in her lap like a living, waiting creature. I told her the basic outline of what I knew: Johanna hadn't been heard from in twenty-four hours, and the photographer couldn't be reached, either. I also told her what Johanna had been writing about.

"Johanna would have called," Elina said when I'd finished. She spoke so quietly that I had to repeat the sentence in my mind.

I nodded and looked up at Ahti, who had just come into the room. He was a short, wiry man, a lawyer by trade, meticulous to the point of being comical, but just as likely to surprise you in some situations. A thought occurred to me, and as it did I saw a trace of uncertainty in Ahti's blue, penetrating eyes that disappeared as quickly as it had come.

He looked quickly at me, then gave Elina a longer, more meaningful look. They held each other's gaze for an unusually long time and then, almost in unison, turned their gazes back to me. Elina's brown eyes welled with tears. I'd never seen her cry before, but it didn't surprise me for some reason. Maybe the exaggerated homeyness of the room was a sign that surprises were in the offing.

"We should have told you about this before," Ahti said. He stood with his hands in his pockets behind Elina's chair. Tears glistened on her face.

"What?" I asked.

Elina quickly wiped her eyes as if the tears were in her way.

"We're leaving," she said. "We're going north."

"We have a year's lease on an apartment in a little town up there," Ahti said.

"A year?" I said. "What about when the year's over?"

Elina's eyes filled with tears again. Ahti stroked her hair, she lifted her hand and held his. The eyes of both wandered the room, unable to latch onto anything. A more paranoid person might have thought that they were being evasive about something, but what could they have to be evasive about?

"We don't know," Ahti said. "But it can't be any worse than living here. I lost my job for good six months ago. Elina hasn't had regular teaching work for a couple of years now."

"You haven't said anything about it," I remarked quietly.

"We didn't want to because we thought things would get better."

We sat for a moment in silence. The smell of fresh coffee floated into the room. I wasn't the only one who noticed it.

"I'll go see if the coffee's done brewing," Ahti said with audible relief.

Elina wiped her eyes on the sleeve of her sweatshirt. The loose sleeve wrapped around her wrist and she had to straighten it with her other hand.

"We really believed we would think of something," she

said, again so quietly that I had to lean forward to make out the words that fell from her lips, "that there was some solution, that this had all been some kind of horrible, sudden crisis that would work itself out and life would go on like before."

I didn't know if she was talking about their situation or the whole world's, but it probably didn't make any difference.

Ahti came back with the coffeepot. His movements were as smooth and precise as always as he poured the coffee into cups painted with flowers like mementos of a time forever lost. Which, of course, they were.

"Have you sold this place?" I asked, waving a hand and looking around to indicate the apartment. Ahti shook his head.

"No," he said quietly.

"Tell him the truth, Ahti," Elina said, wiping away the two or three more tears trickling down her cheeks with her sweatshirt sleeve.

Ahti sat at the other end of the sofa and pulled his cup closer, obviously going over the matter in his mind before speaking.

"Who would buy this place?" he said, sitting up straighter. "There are holes in the roof, there's water in the basement, mold everywhere, rats and cockroaches. The electricity goes out all the time, and so does the water. The city's about to collapse. No one has any money, and the ones who do sure don't want to move in here. There are no more investors, and even if there were, why pay rent when you can live someplace for free? And who really believes things are going to get better?"

Elina stared straight ahead, not crying anymore.

"We believed," she said quietly, looking at Ahti.

"We believed for a really long time," he agreed.

I couldn't think of anything to say. I drank my coffee, watching the steam rise from it, warming my hands on the cup.

"Johanna's certain to turn up," Elina said suddenly, waking me from my thoughts.

I looked up at Elina, then at Ahti. He was nodding to her, as if to confirm what she'd said, and stopped suddenly when he noticed me staring at him. I didn't let that, or the trace of uncertainty I saw again in his eyes, trip me up. I knew that if I didn't ask, I might regret it.

"Ahti, I could help you out with a little money and buy something from you at the same time."

He hesitated a second. He was obviously searching for words.

"I don't know what we could have that you—"

"You like to go shooting sometimes," I said.

He looked almost surprised. He glanced at Elina, who didn't say anything, but nodded. Ahti leaned forward.

"Why not?" he said, getting up. "I don't need both of the shotguns, and I only need one pistol. And I doubt there's anyone who'd turn me in if I sold you a gun."

I followed him into the bedroom. Large, nearly full duffel bags stood in front of the open, ransacked closets. There were clothes on the bed, headboard, and two chairs, and piled on the floor in front of the bags. Ahti went around the bed, stopped in front of a freestanding dark wood cabinet, and opened the door with a key. In the cabinet were two shotguns, a small rifle, and three pistols.

"Take your pick," he said, pointing at one pistol and then the other. There was a touch of the salesman in the gesture, which seemed unnecessary under the circumstances. "A nine-millimeter Heckler and Koch USP or a Glock seventeen, also nine millimeters."

Then he pointed at a steel revolver above them, and he didn't look the slightest bit like a salesman. He looked like a man who had made a decision.

"The Smith and Wesson is for me."

I took down the nearest pistol, the Heckler and Koch.

"That's a nice piece. Made in Germany, back when they still made things in Germany."

The gun was surprisingly light.

"Six hundred sixty-seven grams," Ahti said, before I could ask. "Holds eighteen shots in the clip."

He took out a box from the lower shelf. It clinked as he picked it up.

"You can have these, too, of course. Fifty rounds."

I looked at the box and at the gun in my hand. They both seemed completely out of place in this ordinary bedroom. I had to act fast, before I changed my mind.

"Do you have a backpack?" I asked.

He found a small black backpack in one of the jumbled closets. Its ordinariness, its plain old gymbagness, contrasted shockingly with its intended contents.

"No extra charge. Least I can do."

I gave him the money. He put it in his pocket without counting it and without looking at me. I looked again at the pistol in my right hand and the box of cartridges in my left. Ahti saw my befuddlement.

"I'll show you," he laughed, and took the gun from me.

With quick, practiced movements he dropped open the clip, filled it from the box, and pushed it back into place. He seemed to be in his element.

"Ready," he said. "This is the safety and this is the trigger. Don't aim it at anyone you don't intend to shoot. Or maybe that doesn't matter anymore."

He tried to smile, but there was no energy in it. His smile

congealed on his lips and gave his face a helpless look. He realized it himself.

"The coffee's getting cold," he said quickly. "Let's go drink it."

I thought about how suddenly things had changed. How long ago was it that we had spent dinners together, drank wine, planned our futures? We were going to take trips, I was going to write books, Johanna would write better articles than ever, and Ahti was going to start his own law office and—of course, naturally—a family, with Elina.

The change had crept into our lives gradually, but now it was all coming to an end suddenly, in one great crash.

Elina sat in her chair, not touching her coffee. I sank into the sofa and tried to think of something appropriate to say. It wasn't easy because I had only one thing to talk about. Ahti must have sensed it: "I hope you find Johanna," he said.

I realized that that was my only hope in the world. I understood it with a clarity that penetrated me like warmth or cold and made me remember everything good that I might lose. A lump rose in my throat. I had to get out of there.

"I hope you like it up north," I said. "I hope everything works out for you up there. I'm sure it will. A year's a long time. You'll find some work, earn some money. It'll be fine."

There was something missing from my words. But words weren't the biggest thing missing. It felt like we all heard it and—above all—felt it. And I didn't really know how long I could continue speaking, so I got up from the sofa without looking at either of them.

"Elina, Johanna will call you as soon as she can."

I went into the foyer. Ahti followed me and stood in the darkest corner of the room. I heard Elina's steps on the wood floor and then she was standing in front of me, tears in her eyes again. She came to me and gave me a hug.

"Tell Johanna everything will be OK," she said, her arms still around me. "And tell her that we never meant any harm."

I wasn't sure what she meant by that, but I didn't want to linger so I didn't ask for an explanation.

6

THE RAIN HAD GAINED IN STRENGTH. IT CAME DOWN FROM THE sky in broad swaths of fat, heavy drops that fell to the asphalt and splattered as if in a tantrum, turning the surrounding city shiny, black, and wet. There was something sour in the smell of it, almost rancid. I stood for a moment in the arch of the entryway trying to decide what my next step should be, thinking about where I was and where I was going. It was nine-thirty. I'd lost my wife and drunk who knows how many cups of black coffee. There was no way I was going to be able to get to sleep.

I could hear a fight coming from where the laughter had been before, the sound of shattered glass followed a moment later by the laughing woman's shrieking, cursing protests. I pulled the hood of my parka up, tightened the straps of the backpack, and set out.

I kept my eyes focused straight ahead. The rain stung cold on my skin. I turned into Fredrikinkatu and had taken a few steps when I heard a car horn toot once, then twice. The sound was coming from across the street. I pulled my hood aside enough to see who was honking: the same young North African man who had driven me here from Herttoniemi.

The taxi was sitting in the center of the dark block with the motor on, and it looked significantly drier and warmer inside than it was on the sidewalk. In a few seconds I was sitting firmly in the backseat and asking him to take me south this time.

He had a name and a history: Hamid. Been in Finland for six months. Why had he waited for me? Because I was a paying customer. I couldn't blame him. Not many people want to work for free.

Hamid liked Finland. Here, at least, there was some possibility of making good—he might even be able to start a family here.

I listened to his fast-flowing, broken English and watched him in profile. A narrow, light-brown face, alert, nut-brown eyes in the rearview mirror; quick hands on the steering wheel. Then I looked at the city flashing by, the flooded streets glistening, puddles the size of ponds, shattered windows, doors pried from their hinges, cars burned black, and people wandering in the rain. Where I saw doom, Hamid saw hope.

We came to the end of Lönnrotinkatu, crossed the shore road, and headed for Jätkäsaari.

Hamid drove slowly now. He had stopped talking and turned the stereo up. The music thudding and twitching from the speakers was some sort of combination of hip-hop and North African music. A man's voice, speaking a thousand words a minute in an unknown language, moved rhythmically over it.

When Hamid asked me where to go, I said straight ahead. I couldn't think what else to do. I opened Johanna's documents on my phone again and went quickly through her memos. I opened the sound file, too, with Johanna and me edited out, and asked Hamid to hook my phone up to his speakers. He said it would cost extra. I said I'd pay extra. He said in advance. I handed him the phone and some money. He smiled broadly, folded the bill and put it in his pocket, then plugged the phone into the speakers.

The thousand-words-a-minute man fell silent, replaced by the murmur.

Hamid looked at me curiously, obviously reassessing me.

I nodded: this was what I wanted to hear.

We came to the end of the road—ahead on the right was the bridge to Lauttasaari, ahead on the left darkness, and behind us, apartment buildings. Hamid asked where next. I pointed to the closed waterfront café and the parking lot behind it.

The café was dark on the inside and lit up on the outside. Its large rectangular windows were intact and clean, and there wasn't much trash around the place, either. It was as if we'd driven into another world in just fifteen minutes.

I told Hamid this was a good spot and asked him to turn off the motor so I could listen. I passed him another bill. He turned off the motor and let the murmur drift through the car and disappear into the darkness. I opened the window and asked him to slowly lower the volume.

One murmur faded, another took its place.

Maybe.

Just maybe?

A firm maybe?

Maybe this was where Johanna had called me from.

I asked Hamid to wait, took my phone, and got out of the car. The wind blowing off the sea immediately grabbed my hair and clothes. It ripped and tore like it was trying to get a good grip on me. This close to the shore, its hands would have been wet even without the rain.

I pulled up my hood and held the phone to my ear under it, sheltered from the rain, and let it play the murmuring sound again. I raised and lowered the volume as I walked north along the shore, looking at the six-, seven-, and eight-story waterfront houses. Not knowing where to begin, I tried to see and hear parallels among what may have been unrelated things: the last phone call, the sounds in it that might have been wind and waves, the Healer's coordinates that Johanna had plotted, and my own instinct and hope. I relied on these as I walked along the rainy, windy point, my shoes wet through, the soles of my feet aching with cold.

The houses along the shore seemed to be in unusually good condition: there were lights in many of the apartments, which was almost a small miracle, for at least two reasons. We were near the shore, an area that often flooded. We were also in a wealthy neighborhood. In a lot of other places that meant that the residents had gone north already—got out while the getting was good, whatever that means these days.

There was a steel stairway built into the vertically split side of a large rock. I climbed up the stairs and came to a little platform surrounded by a waist-high steel railing. I found a pair of binoculars fixed to the seaside, pointed out toward open water. You could probably see a long way with them on a sunny day. At the moment, you couldn't see anything.

I turned around. The waterfront café was a couple of hundred meters away and the nearest house about fifty meters. I lowered the phone from my ear. I listened.

The rough, salty smell of the sea and the rhythm of the waves spilling against the shore was calming and soothing in the midst of the wind and rain. Some say the sound of the sea was impressed into our genes long ago. Some say it will one day, once more, press us under.

I went down the stairs and headed back toward the taxi.

When I'd got about halfway there, a hundred meters from the rock and a hundred meters from the cab, I suddenly found myself in a spotlight's beam. I stopped and heard heavy footsteps coming from the direction of the light. Then the footsteps stopped.

The men were holding bright, powerful flashlights, which they seemed to have lifted onto their shoulders. They didn't say anything. I didn't say anything. Only the sea and the wind spoke, overlapping murmurs. Neither of the men took a step forward. They stood in front of me, one to the right and one to the left. They had apparently been trained to stand this way, far enough from each other that the beams of their flashlights crossed where I stood.

The brightness of the light forced me to lower my head. I didn't see the club until it hit my left side, near the kidney.

I fell to the ground and gulped for breath, paralyzed with pain, held fast in place.

"What are you doing here?" I heard from above me.

I tried to say that I didn't mean any harm, I was just looking around. Before I could speak, I felt a steel-toed army boot smash into my stomach. The last vestiges of oxygen disappeared. The blinding beams of light spun wildly.

"What are you hanging around here for?"

"What kind of bum are you?"

"We don't need any fucking refugees around here."

I tried to say something. Spit gurgled out of my throat, not sufficient for words.

"Beggar."

A kick to the ribs.

"Loser."

A club to the right kidney.

"Fag."

A kick to the groin.

I couldn't see anything, could hear only words oozing with hate. I turned onto my stomach. Another blow exploded in the middle of my back like an angry stone.

"You're lucky there ain't more of us today."

"You're getting off easy."

"You coulda been killed."

Laughter. A club struck my left ear. It turned hot and deaf at the same time. More laughter.

Then a third voice, younger, speaking English: "Back off, or I'll shoot."

The beams of light disappeared.

"Go now. Go away, or I'll kill you."

Heavy steps. Moving away this time.

"Get going."

Lighter steps. Hands grabbing my coat, lifting me.

"Get up."

I tried to stand. It wasn't easy. I leaned against something.

"Into the car."

I fell onto something, first sitting, then lying down. A door slammed behind me. The world lurched; I rolled onto my back, then onto my side. Something hit me in the forehead.

"Now let's get out of here."

Of course. I was in the car. In Hamid's taxi.

"They almost killed you."

I rolled onto my stomach. I leaned my head forward and vomited onto the floor.

"Shit. Now we really have to hurry."

I tried to stay conscious. I tried to hold on to the door handle. I tried to open my eyes. It seemed like no matter what I tried, I failed.

"We'll be there in fifteen minutes. Just fifteen more minutes."

Fifteen minutes. To where?

7

I HELD JOHANNA IN MY ARMS, BREATHED IN THE SCENT OF HER NECK and kissed her warm lips. She let out a little laugh, pulled her face away, and looked into my eyes. I was about to say something, but then she was back in my arms again, laying her head on my chest. I stroked her hair, letting it flow through my fingers, and rested my other hand on the back of her neck. It was slender and graceful, radiating heat at the roots of her hair.

I could feel in my fingertips the places where the muscles attached, the delicate point where everything, where life itself, was connected. Johanna lifted her head. I looked into her eyes again and saw the green reflections in them. I pulled her closer and held her tight against me. She was small and soft like she always is in the morning. She turned off the alarm clock and snuggled close, put her arm across my chest, laid her forehead against my cheek and nearly fell asleep again, snuffled, said something sweet and silly.

I held her there, knowing that if I let her go I would let her go forever. I smelled her hair, breathing in its fragrance and trying to store it all away and remember how she really smelled, remember it for a long time. She breathed evenly. Silence surrounded us and we were safe. We belonged to each other.

Then she gave a start, like she sometimes did when she was falling asleep. Someone was pulling her away. I pulled back, clutching her closer to me, but that someone was strong and persistent. I held on to her. I wouldn't let go. I tried to see her face, but it was turned downward. My grasp came loose. That unknown someone finally got hold of her and she sank away out of my arms into the darkness. When she had disappeared completely from my sight and only emptiness was left, I felt a shivering cold. I shook, and my hands reached out to grasp at nothing.

The light changed to a deep red, cursive neon behind a thin curtain. I tried to read it for some time from left to right before I realized that I was looking at it backward. I finally managed to make it out from right to left: kebab-pizzeria.

I lifted my hand to my left ear, which was itching, and I felt a rustling wad of bandage, held on with tape. I was lying on my side with my weight on my right arm, which had gone completely numb. I pulled my arm out from under me, grabbed hold of the edge of whatever it was I was lying on, and sat up.

I was in some sort of back room or storage area. My mouth tasted like blood and metal. I sat where I was, took a few deep breaths, shook my numb arm gingerly. There was a pain in my back whenever I breathed.

I heard a language foreign to me on the other side of the curtain—first a man's voice, then a woman's. I remembered my dream, felt a sense of panic, and took my phone out of my pocket. The display was dark. Either it had been hit by a club or the battery was dead. My panic grew.

I tried to get up, but my legs wouldn't hold me, and I collapsed back to where I'd been sitting.

I fixed my gaze on the red text glowing behind the curtain and managed to remain upright. I breathed for a moment until I was sure that I wouldn't get dizzy, and looked around me. A gray cement room, cardboard boxes and junk along the walls, plastic sacks full of soft drink bottles in the doorway, some full, some empty, and a chair with the backpack I'd got from Ahti slung over it. It was less than two meters away.

I got to my feet again and—made wiser by my previous attempt—used the wall for support. I got the backpack and sat down again. The gun lay in my hand as the pack fell to the floor.

The voices behind the curtain paused.

I held the pistol on my lap as the curtain was pulled aside. I recognized Hamid in spite of the red glow behind him that left his face in darkness and formed a halo around his head, softening his outline.

"Take it easy," he said.

I shook my head, opened my mouth, and moved my tongue, but I couldn't get any sound to come out.

"Water," I heard Hamid say.

A moment later the curtain was pulled completely to one side. Into the room came a woman with a pitcher of water in one hand and a glass in the other. She filled the glass, set the pitcher on the floor, and handed the glass to me.

I drank as if it were my first taste of water. Half of it slopped down my chest, the other half I coughed back up. Swallowing was going to take some practice. I did better with the second glass—the woman didn't need to back up to avoid a spray of water this time.

She was about thirty years old, brown-eyed, with slightly lighter brown skin than Hamid. She had long black hair twisted into a bun on the back of her head and large silver earrings that shone brightly. She was wearing dark jeans, a yellowish hooded sweatshirt, and a startlingly white apron. She handed me my backpack.

"My cousin," Hamid said, nodding in her direction.

He came closer and pointed to my ear.

"She knows what she's doing."

I touched the wad of paper and tape. For that ear the world was full of rustlings and raspings. It didn't hurt, though, so perhaps it was wisest to be grateful. And I was. I said so to Hamid.

"Yes," he said with a smile. "They almost did you in."

The woman also smiled. I tried to.

"Thanks," I said to her. First in Finnish, then in English.

"I speak Finnish," she said. "It's all right."

"Tapani," I said, extending my hand.

"Nina."

Her hand was warm and narrow in mine, and I held on to it longer than was necessary for a handshake. Its slenderness immediately reminded me of the dream I'd just had about my wife, whose hand was just as smooth and delicate. My mind was flooded with memories, and in all of them I was touching Johanna. On the street at night coming home from the movies, under the table at a boring dinner party when no one was watching, walking her to work on an early summer morning.

Nina noticed.

"I'm sorry," I said.

Hamid intervened: "You're in some kind of difficulty."

It was close enough to the truth, so I nodded.

"Can you tell me about it?"

Why not? Provided he would tell me where I was.

"You're in Kallio," he said.

I told him that my wife had disappeared and I had to keep looking for her. The gun was mine, and I would pay Hamid for having returned it to me. He kept his eyes on me all the time I was speaking.

Nina got up from the chair, went out into the restaurant, and came back carrying her purse. She took out a packet of painkillers and handed it to me.

"Thank you," I said, taking out two tablets and swallowing them with some water.

Next Hamid went into the restaurant, clattered around for a moment, and came back carrying a cup and saucer.

"Tea. With lots of sugar."

The tea was as dark as coffee, burning hot, and so sweet it sent a stab through my teeth. I drank the whole cup in a few swallows. I felt the hot liquid in my throat and a moment later in my stomach.

When I was sure the tea would stay down, I got up and stood for a moment. I took a few tottering steps toward the door and went out into the restaurant. The room was the size of a small office. Half the space was taken up by an open kitchen and buffet counter that stretched along one wall. The other half was set aside for three small tables. The wooden chairs around the tables were empty. A television on the wall was showing a report about a wildfire.

"Is this the local news?" I asked.

Nina shook her head.

"Our home country," Hamid said.

I looked at the fire again. It looked like all the other fires in the world.

"I'm sorry," I said to Hamid.

"Me, too," he said.

Nina picked up the remote from the counter and changed the channel. The Helsinki area information station reported news of the capital continuously. I asked her to call up the latest news broadcast. She pressed the remote.

I took out my phone and asked for a charger. Hamid snapped up the phone and took it behind the counter.

I sat in one of the restaurant's chairs and looked at the clock on the wall: twelve past one. I felt weak and sick. Ideas came into my mind, but I didn't want to follow them to their conclusions. Most of the thoughts revolved around Johanna, and the mere idea that something might have happened to her like what had just happened to me hurt more than the beating I'd taken.

The local news didn't offer any more clues. Armed robberies had increased—they were being committed in the daytime now, and closer to the city center. A skyscraper in central Pasila had been set on fire earlier in the evening. Traffic from the Russian border to the capital was jammed again. There was also good news: The metro tunnels had been pumped out, and the metro was back up and running. They had also increased the number of armed guards there.

But none of that was any help to me.

Hamid sat on the other side of the table.

"I'm sure things will get better," he said when I turned away from the television and looked at him.

I STOOD FOR A moment in front of the pizzeria, breathing in the night's thin air, feeling it in my throat, and keeping my eyes on the trees that stood stock-still behind the library, silently waiting for spring, for warmth and new life, in the middle of the winter, in the middle of the night, glistening with rain, their limbs dripping. The earth beneath them was numbingly cold and would be for months yet, but the trees didn't let their nerves get to them, they didn't tremble or blame anyone for the unpleasantness of their situation. I was awakened from this lesson when Hamid backed the taxi around the corner and stopped in front of me.

I turned my phone back on in the taxi. No sign of Johanna. I took out a tissue and wiped my earlobe. The wound had opened again when I washed my face. The tissue turned dark red in seconds. I took a new one out of my pocket and held it against my ear.

We drove north to avoid the roads closed due to the high-rise fire in Pasila and made it to the police station without any trouble. Hamid stopped the car a few hundred meters before he reached the gates, and I handed him who knows how many bills. I hadn't calculated how much the fare would be. He had saved my life, so I felt I ought to pay a little extra. I asked him to wait. If I didn't return in an hour, he could go look for another fare.

I walked as upright as the pain in my back would allow me, shoved the bloody tissue in my pocket, and adjusted my face into as friendly and neutral an expression as I could without a mirror. In spite of all that my way was blocked as soon as I got to the gate in the fence that surrounded the police station.

No, I don't have a pass.

No, no one is expecting me.

I explained that I'd come to see Harri Jaatinen, chief inspector of the violent crimes unit, and that I was there concerning the man known as the Healer. The young policeman, in a heavy armored vest and helmet, with an assault rifle in his hands and eyes that kept darting from side to side, listened to me for a moment, then walked to the guard's booth without saying a word, waited, and opened the gate.

I was directed to the security checkpoint, where they took my phone and gave me an ID badge to pin to my chest. After security I walked into a building with a large foyer full of people and only one empty seat.

Across from me sat a wealthy-looking, well-dressed couple roughly the age of Johanna and me. The woman was half in the man's lap, sniffling quietly. Her fist clasped a tissue, and her face was twisted and blotched with red. The man's pale face was pointed straight ahead, and the empty, frozen look in his eyes was unchanging as he mechanically moved his hand over her back.

I closed my eyes and waited.

8

"TAPANI LEHTINEN?"

I opened my eyes.

"If you're reporting a theft, robbery, or assault, take a number at the first window."

Harri Jaatinen was amazingly similar in person to the way he seemed in the news clips—just as tall and chiseled as he was in those painful close-ups. I got up and shook his hand. He was quite a bit older than me—nearer to sixty than fifty, with dark gray at his temples, in his mustache, and in his eyes. He reminded me of Dr. Phil, the American psychologist on the old television show. But it took only a few words of conversation to easily distinguish where Dr. Phil ended and Inspector Jaatinen began. Where Dr. Phil would have coaxed and flattered with artificial empathy, Jaatinen's tone was dry, gruff, and unapologetic. It was impossible to imagine that voice dithering, sentimental, or fawning—it was a voice made for pronouncements, statements of fact. His handshake was the same: straightforward and professional.

I instinctively touched the bandage on my ear. It hadn't occurred to me that it might seem to be my reason for being here. I shook my head.

"I'm here about the Healer. I believe my wife, the journalist Johanna Lehtinen, has been in touch with you about the case."

Jaatinen seemed to remember and understand immediately what I was talking about. He switched his weight from one leg to the other.

"That case and many others," he said, and I couldn't quite tell from his expression whether he was pleased and faintly smiling, or vexed by the memory. Then he said, "Do you want a cup of coffee?"

The coffee was acrid, but warm. The stark room contained a desk, two chairs, and Jaatinen's computer.

I quickly told him everything that had happened over the past twenty-four hours: Johanna's disappearance, how I had found out about her investigation, and, of course, my own investigations, which had resulted in the bandage on my ear, a back that was black and blue, and a crazy theory about waves on the seashore.

"Johanna's a good reporter," Jaatinen said. "She's been a lot of help to us." His voice didn't rise or fall and had no shades of color or tone. He didn't take sides or make commitments. But it was a surprisingly pleasant voice to listen to. "As you no doubt know, we're short of staff at the moment. I'm sure you understand that I can't spare any staff to search for your wife. Or for anyone else."

"That's not what I'm looking for," I said. "I want to know more about the Healer, because that's how I can find Johanna."

Jaatinen shook his head sharply.

"That's not at all certain."

"It's all I've got. And the police have nothing to lose,

whether I find her or not. In any case, you'll have one more man investigating the murders. Everybody wins."

Jaatinen measured me with a glance and didn't answer right away. Maybe he was calculating my trustworthiness, or comparing me in his mind to the thousand other people offering or asking for help that he must run across in his profession. I sat in my chair and tried to look as forthright as possible, tried to look like I'd be a lot of help to him. The bandage on my ear probably didn't reinforce that impression.

"We have DNA tests from only some of the cases because the lab is overbooked and understaffed, and the equipment is starting to wear out. Anyway, there are DNA tests from the most recent case, the murder in Eira. What I'm about to tell you is absolutely confidential until you hear otherwise. I shouldn't be telling you this, but Johanna was a great help to us, and to me particularly, in solving those kidnappings three years ago."

He took a sip of coffee and glanced at his cup with a satisfied look. I was perplexed, and tasted mine again. It was almost undrinkable.

"We have one suspect, the same person who's suspected in the first murder, the one in Tapiola. We got a DNA sample in that case, too, and we even got it to the lab for testing, which happens less and less nowadays."

He took another mouthful of coffee. He was enjoying his so much that he was willingly lingering over it before swallowing.

"So. We compared the samples to the national DNA bank and got a name. There was only one problem."

His gray-blue eyes shone in the poorly lit room. He looked all of a sudden like he was sitting much closer to me than I'd realized. Either that or the room around us had shrunk and the walls were pushing us closer together.

"The man in question died in the flu epidemic five years ago."

"OK," I said after a little pause, trying my best to make myself comfortable in the suddenly confined space.

He put his coffee down and pushed it away from him, dropped his gaze to his elbows leaning on the desk, and scooted them forward, too. If the desk had been a living thing it would have been crying in pain.

"The suspect was about to graduate from medical school. Pasi Tarkiainen. Died at home."

"So?"

Jaatinen's expression was unchanged, and the pitch of his voice remained the same. Apparently he was used to explaining things to people slower than himself.

"So we have a dead medical student who left traces of himself that were found on the victims," he said. "And he may be using the name 'the Healer.' "

"There must be some explanation."

He seemed to be of the same opinion; an indentation appeared between his lower lip and the tip of his outstretched chin that seemed to say: Exactly. Quite. That is the point.

"Of course there is. But we don't have enough investigators to find out what it is. We had three detectives officially resign yesterday, and one of them was assigned to this case. Last week two of my employees didn't come to work, and it looks like they're gone for good, since they took their weapons with them but left their security passes. And this bunch has a calling for the job—I can only imagine what the situation's like in other departments."

He drummed his fingers on the desk a few times and sharpened his gaze.

"All our time goes to recording new cases. There's no time for investigation because new, and worse, cases are constantly arriving. We go as fast as we can and we're still at square one. It's no wonder people give up. Maybe I should leave, too, while I still can. But where would I go? That's what I can't figure out."

"Did Johanna know about this?" I asked. "About Pasi Tarkiainen?"

Jaatinen leaned back and sized me up again, me and the whole situation.

"Probably not. Unless she found out through her own research. Our department's not as airtight as it used to be. After all, here I am talking to you. But did she know? I don't think she knew."

I shifted my position in the chair, trying to throw my left leg over my right, but the pain in my lower back stopped me like a wall. It was as if someone had taken a screwdriver directly to the nerve. I let out a squeak and put the leg back where it was before.

"Do you know who they were?" Jaatinen asked.

"The ones who clobbered me?"

He nodded. In a friendly way this time, I thought. I shrugged. It was of absolutely no importance, I thought. "If I had to guess, I'd say they were from some private security company, paid professional sadists. There are still people living in those houses, and they can afford to pay someone to keep the place clean."

"The only sector that's growing," Jaatinen said. "We've had a lot of people defect. They want to try to earn enough to go north. But the space up there isn't unlimited. And life up north can't be much easier or more delightful than it is here."

I had to get the discussion back on track. I was looking for Johanna, not pondering convulsions in the labor market.

"Let's assume that you could investigate the Healer and Tarkiainen," I said. "Where would you begin?"

Jaatinen seemed to have expected this question. He didn't think for even a second before saying, "I'd look for Tarkiainen. Dead or not."

"How?" I asked.

"With the information you have, some instinct, and a bit of luck. You'll need all of it. The evidence indicates that Tarkiainen is alive. Somewhere there are people who know him. I'd be surprised if they weren't right around the corner. I have a feeling the killer knows the areas he's active in very well. The same would apply to the people around him. I would look for old friends of his—workmates, neighbors, golf buddies, kindred spirits. One of them might still be in contact with him. He might even go to the same pub he used to."

Jaatinen was quiet for a moment and seemed to purposely leave the obvious question hanging in the air.

"You don't believe that Tarkiainen's dead?"

He didn't need to wrestle with his answer.

"No," he said in a dry and implacable voice.

We talked for a few more minutes, and I had the feeling he was still keeping me at a distance. He had told me a lot, but not everything.

I DIDN'T PRESS HIM. Nor could I bring myself to ask him directly what he thought Johanna's chances were, but we did talk about the kidnapping case three years earlier that she had helped to solve, thanks to which two girls, aged six and eight, though permanently traumatized, had been returned alive. I could tell that Jaatinen hoped this chat would encourage me. I did my best to accept whatever crumbs I could get from it.

After a moment of silence, he got up and pulled up his dark suit pants. I did the same with my jeans. There was another sharp pain in my back. We shook hands and I thanked him for his time. He said, "We'll keep trying," and I said, "Yes we will." We were at the door before his choice of words registered.

I turned to him and asked, "Why do you keep trying?"

For a moment, he didn't look like Dr. Phil. He looked like someone else—maybe himself.

"Why," he said. It was more a statement than a question.

His face had a look that was familiar by now, the faintest trace of a little joy—or was it annoyance?

"There's still a chance to do more good than harm here. And I am a policeman. I believe in what I do. Until I have evidence to the contrary."

9

"YOU'RE THE STRANGEST PERSON I KNOW," JOHANNA ONCE SAID AS she came and rested her hands on the back of my neck. "You can sit there for hours staring at emptiness and still look completely focused."

"That's just it," I answered, rousing myself from my thoughts. "I'm not staring at emptiness. I'm working."

"Take a break once in a while," she said with a laugh. "So you don't wear yourself out."

She swung herself astride my lap, her legs dangling above the floor, and pressed her lips against mine for a long time, then laughed again.

Life's most significant moments are so fleetingly short and so much a matter of course when they're happening that they're greeted with a grunt or a smile. It's only later that you realize you should have said something, been grateful, told a person you love her. I would have given anything now to feel Johanna's gentle hand caress my face or her warm, full, almost dry lips on my temple.

I sat in the backseat of the taxi exhausted, staring into the dark, and didn't like what I was thinking. Hamid asked where to. Nowhere yet, I answered. I needed a minute to breathe. So we sat in the car in the dark, not far from the Pasila police station. Hamid turned up the heat, then turned it down. It seemed balance was a challenge even in this task.

The rain was so soft and light now that you didn't realize it was a cold winter rain until you were soaked through and shaking with the chill. The digital clock made to look analog on the dashboard said it was half past two. Hamid moved his lips in time to the softly playing music, glanced at me in the rearview mirror, fiddled with his phone, and was clearly bored. I opened my phone to the map Johanna had made.

Tapiola, Lauttasaari, Kamppi, Kulosaari.

Tuomarinkylä, Pakila, Kumpula, Töölö, Punavuori.

West–East / North–South.

I searched for information on Pasi Tarkiainen, but everything I found was more than five years old. There were at least four former addresses: in Kallio, Töölö, Tapiola, and Munkkiniemi. He had worked at doctor's offices in Töölö, Eira, and right downtown, on Kaivokatu.

I remembered what Jaatinen had said. I looked through the lists again. Töölö was on every one of them.

I did an image search, too. The picture was from ten years ago. The young Pasi Tarkiainen didn't look like a murderer. He looked happy, like a bright, optimistic medical student. His smile was so infectious that I almost smiled back. But when I looked closely at the photo, I saw something else. The eyes behind the glasses were ever so slightly mismatched to the dimples in his glowing cheeks. They were older than the face that surrounded them—serious, nervous even. His light hair was short, gelled, and styled in sawtooth bangs. In spite of his broad smile he looked like a man who took things very seriously.

I put down the phone and leaned against the headrest. For a moment I was somewhere else. Closing my eyes was like a time machine. I could go anywhere, forward or back, in seconds.

Johanna.

Always and everywhere.

I opened my eyes and was back in a taxi with a North African driver, surrounded by rain.

I gave Hamid an address, and he pulled onto the road with relief. We descended the hill from Pasila toward the zoological gardens. The windows of the Aurora Hospital reflected bright spotlights like a long row of mirrors. The hospital was guarded by soldiers, particularly around the infectious disease clinic. There were rumors that the guards were there for two reasons: to keep the public out, and to keep the patients in. The same rumors spoke of Ebola, plague, a strain of diphtheria resistant to every treatment, tuberculosis, malaria. The trees of Keskuspuisto formed a wall of gloom behind the hospital. There was no reliable count of how many people were living in the park, permanently or temporarily. The highest estimate was ten thousand. It was as good a guess as any.

We drove past the hockey arena, where hundreds of people flocked, even at this hour of the night. The arena filled with transients every evening—it had become a permanent emergency shelter.

A tram stood dark at the corner of Mannerheimintie and Nordenskiöldinkatu like a great green forgotten thing, like someone had simply walked away and left it there. Hamid was quiet. He drove around the tram and continued down the street toward Töölö.

We stopped on Museokatu. Tarkiainen had lived at 24 Museokatu, and the director of a plastic packaging company and his family of five had been slain at Vänrikki Stoolin katu number 3. The distance from Tarkiainen's former front door to the scene of the crime was about a hundred meters.

I didn't tell Hamid why we were parked on Museokatu—I wasn't sure myself.

I got out of the car, walked to the front of number 24, and looked toward the intersection of Vänrikki Stoolin katu. I felt the rain, first softly on my face, a moment later in swift, freezing drops that slid down into my collar. I looked at the dark, rain-soaked street and then glanced around—I didn't see anything that screamed mass murderer or missing wife.

I walked across to Vänrikki Stoolin katu and looked back to where I'd been. Many of the apartments at Museokatu 24 had a direct view of where I was standing. The windows of the building were dark now except for the topmost floor, where I counted a row of six lighted windows.

I walked back to the cab and was about to get in when I recognized a green and yellow sign a little farther down the street. Why hadn't I thought of that?

I asked Hamid to wait a minute and jogged the hundred meters with my shoulders hunched and my hands in my pockets, as if that could protect me from getting drenched. Memories from years back flooded my mind. They came in no particular order, with no reference to the year or the nature of the events. The one thing they all had in common was that each memory was as unwelcome as the next.

Some things never change, and some things just don't improve with age. The bar looked basically the same as it had ten or fifteen years earlier. Four steps led up from the street and a long counter sat on one side near the door. There were three tables on the right and a dozen in the lounge on the left, and a gap in the wall at the end of the bar. You could see through it into the back room, where there were a few more tables. The place swayed and shook with the sound of music and shouting.

It took effort to make my way through the wall of people to the counter and at least as much effort to get a beer ordered. A pint of beer was slammed down in front of me; I paid for it and tried to see if there was anyone in the bar I knew. The bartenders running back and forth behind the counter weren't familiar, nor was the thin-bearded loudmouth bumming money next to me. He looked remarkably young up close.

I had come to this bar for years, sometimes too regularly. It was on the route I walked to or from downtown back when I lived on Mechelininkatu. That was the time before Johanna. It wasn't a good time.

Patrons at numerous tables had already passed the point where coherent conversation becomes impossible—the only point now was to manage to make a noise at all, to lean on one another and drink some more. I didn't recognize anyone so I continued into the back room.

It was even more poorly ventilated than the front. The smell of liquor and piss intertwined and took command of the air. The people at the tables were complete strangers to me, and I was already turning back when I saw a familiar face through the narrow crack of a half-opened door at the rear of the room. A broad-shouldered bartender that I remembered from ten years before finished stacking a pile of boxes, picked up the top one, walked out of the storage room, and slammed the door shut behind him with one elbow. He noticed me. I gave him a cheerful hello and wished I could remember his name. I couldn't, so my greeting was brief. He continued to the front room with the case of vodka in his arms.

I followed him and shouldered my way up to the counter. I put my beer down on the glass countertop and put my hand in something dark and sticky. I greeted the bartender again. He noticed me and came to stand in front of me behind the counter. He hadn't really changed in ten years; his face was a little more angular, it was true, and there were deep lines in his cheeks on either side of his mouth. His eyes had dimmed and become more expectant, as sometimes happens with age. But his ponytail was still there, his shoulders still spread broad, and the stubble on his chin was the same dark, scruffy mat as it was long ago.

I took my phone out of my pocket.

"I used to come here," I said.

"I remember," he said, and added, with a certain emphasis, "vaguely."

"My wife disappeared."

"That I don't remember."

"It didn't happen here," I said.

He was looking at me now the way he must have looked at most of his customers. He knew very well that there was no point in trying to have a conversation with a drunk about anything more complicated than an order of beer. His face held a completely neutral, closed expression; this was the end of the discussion as far as he was concerned. As he was turning away, I raised my hand.

"Wait," I said, and he turned back toward me. "I'm looking for my wife, and also for another person, a man."

I clicked open the image of Pasi Tarkiainen, enlarged it, and handed the phone to the bartender. The phone shrank in his hand to the size of a matchbox.

"Have you ever seen this guy here?" I asked.

He looked up and handed the phone back to me. The edges of his mouth were curled and his eyes widened ever so slightly.

"Never," he said. But a fleeting, non-neutral expression flashed in his face.

I looked at him for a moment, trying to grasp the hint of something that I'd just seen in his eyes.

"He lived around here," I said. "I believe he's been in here many times."

The bartender waved a hand in my direction. His arm was big enough that he could have reached my nose from where he stood.

"I believe you've been in here many times, and all I remember is the time years ago when we had to carry you to a taxi."

I put my glass down and managed to get my hand stuck to the counter again.

"Thanks for that," I said, searching the length of the bar for something to wipe my hand on. I didn't see anything that would be of service, so I left it in its natural state.

I glanced at the picture shining from my phone and turned the screen toward him once more. He didn't look at it. But the stillness of his gaze seemed to require effort from him; he wasn't as cool and relaxed as he'd been at the beginning of our conversation.

"What if I told you this guy was dead?"

He shrugged his shoulders. The impression was like the lifting and lowering of a fortress wall.

"Do you want something to drink? If not, I'll go serve somebody who does."

"He died five years ago," I said. "In the big flu epidemic."

"A lot of people died back then."

"True," I said. "But not very many came back to life."

His hands stopped. He set the bottle of red wine he was holding in his right hand and the glass in his left hand down on the counter in front of him.

"How about I show you the door?" he said.

"I've only had one beer," I said. "But maybe that was just

too much trouble for you. Or are you going to show me the door because of a guy who died of the flu five years ago?"

I showed him Tarkiainen's picture again, and once again he didn't look at it.

"What's your name?" he asked. "No, never mind—I can find that out myself."

He straightened up, adjusted his stance, and towered over me, showing me his shoulders in all their broadness. Whoever invented the word "overbearing" must have had someone like him in mind.

"Why do you want to know my name?" I asked.

He thrust his head forward but left his chin nearly resting on his chest. He looked at me from under his eyebrows, his lined cheeks completely in shadow.

"So I'll know who I'm showing the door. So I can tell the other employees that there's a guy named such-and-such who's not allowed in here."

"Are you going to tell Pasi Tarkiainen the same thing?"

He made a gesture toward the door. A gigantic block of solid muscle with a bald head the same bright, meaty pink color as raw salmon started to head in my direction.

"See you later," I shouted.

I headed for the block of muscle and the door, smelled aftershave a few meters ahead, and braced myself as well as I could for the bouncer to grab me by some part of my body. He looked at the bartender, then stepped aside and let me pass. I didn't look behind me as I went down the stairs to the street and walked back to the taxi.

Half an hour later I was lying in bed staring out at the dark of the night without seeing anything.

I was thinking about Johanna—and trying not to think about her.

The building was quiet. Nothing was moving; it felt like

nothing anywhere was moving. It wasn't until I lay down that I realized how tired I was, how much my body hurt, how hungry I was, and how hopeless I felt. I couldn't bear to turn my face toward Johanna's pillow, let alone pull her blanket over me, although I was shivering under my own.

The rain tapped a rhythm against the windowsill, took a long pause before breaking out in a tight series of dozens of drops, then quieted again. I closed my eyes, listened to the wind and rain, and let my fists open and my muscles relax. Without realizing it, without wanting to, I fell asleep.

ONE DAY BEFORE CHRISTMAS

10

I ROLLED OVER IN BED AND REACHED FOR THE PHONE ON THE NIGHT table. 6:05 a.m. Unknown number. I'd slept without dreaming for almost exactly three hours.

"Tapani Lehtinen," I said, now fully awake as if I hadn't slept at all—or had slept a long time. I'm not sure which it was.

"Lassi Uutela. I assume I don't need to ask if I've called at a bad time."

My heart skipped a beat. Johanna.

"Not at all," I said, trying to keep my voice level. As if controlling my voice could keep everything else under control.

"I have somewhat bad news, which is connected to Johanna in a way. I thought you'd want to know."

"Of course."

"The photographer, Gromov—the one I tried to call last night?"

"Yes."

"He's dead."

I didn't know what to say. I could feel my pulse throbbing in my neck. Soon it had climbed to my temple.

"There's no information about Johanna," Lassi said. "Gromov was found alone, so it may be that it has nothing to do with her."

"Where was he found?" I asked with a gulp.

"He was thrown from a car up north, along Tuusulantie. Apparently he died somewhere else."

"When?"

"I don't know. I was told we may never know because they might not get around to investigating it."

"How did he die?"

"They didn't tell me."

I rubbed my dry eyes, thought for a moment, then asked, "Was he wearing clothes? Was there anything in his pockets?"

Lassi didn't answer right away. I could hear his fingers quite clearly tapping on his keyboard.

"No information," he said. "I do know that he didn't have his camera or telephone with him."

"I was thinking more of memory cards. Photographers sometimes have them in their pockets, don't they?"

Lassi again didn't answer right away.

"Well," he drawled, and I could hear the keyboard clicking again. "I think they would have mentioned that."

"Who? The police?"

"I haven't heard from the police," he said after a short, emphatic pause. "I'm talking about the men from the security company who found him."

I stood up—it hurt so much to straighten my back that it knocked the wind out of me. I grabbed the head of the bed for support.

"The police didn't find him?"

"No," Lassi said. "Some guys from a private security company called and said they were taking him to the morgue. As you know, they have permission to do that now."

"I know, I know," I said, sounding more impatient than I intended. "Sorry, I didn't mean that."

I took a breath and straightened my back again. The pain didn't let up.

"OK," Lassi said. "Am I supposed to understand what you did mean?"

I told him about Johanna's investigations and my own, with particular emphasis on the thrashing I'd been given. I walked into the kitchen as I spoke, got a glass of water, and sat down at the table. When I'd finished talking, Lassi was silent for a moment.

"Of course there's a remote possibility," he began, speaking considerably more slowly, and without the accompanying pounding of a keyboard. He paused a moment as if looking around the room for answers. "It's possible that there's some connection between these events. But I don't yet see what it is."

"Gromov is dead," I said. "And he hardly would have been thrown into a ditch if he'd died in an accident. How do you even know he was found in a ditch? Maybe they killed him someplace, anyplace, and carted him straight off to the morgue."

I noticed that I'd raised my voice. Lassi noticed, too. His tone turned sarcastic.

"Naturally. First they murder him, then they take him to the morgue, and finally they politely call me. Makes perfect sense."

He paused for a moment; I kept silent and took a drink of water. When he spoke again the sarcasm drained word by word from his voice.

"I called because I thought you'd want to know that at least for now, and at least judging by what we know, Johanna's all right. I intend to find out what this is all about by the end of the day. This may come as a surprise to you, but we do still place some value on our reporters and photographers. We take care of our own. As well as we can in these times."

Neither of us spoke for a moment. Maybe the moment of silence was in memory of Gromov.

"Is there anything you intend to do with regard to Johanna?" I asked.

A brief silence.

"What can I do, really?" Lassi said. "What the heck am I supposed to do? I'm losing my staff, losing the paper itself, at an accelerating pace. I don't have any room to move."

I drank the rest of the water, then got up and went to fill the glass again. When the water's running and you don't have to boil it, it feels like your whole life's a little easier. Or it would have felt that way in some other circumstances, at some other time. I put the glass of water down on the counter.

"Anyway," I said. "Thanks for calling."

Lassi's voice was quieter now, and, surprisingly enough, softer.

"I'm sorry, Tapani. I really wish I could help you—and a lot of other people."

"I believe you," I said, trying to sound as sincere as I could. I looked out at the dark morning.

"But these times . . ."

"I know."

"Take care of yourself."

"Thanks," I said. "You, too."

I lowered the phone from my ear and wiped the sweat from both.

I warmed up some oatmeal in the microwave, mixed in a teaspoon of honey, and ate it. I felt a little better. I immediately made myself another helping and turned on Johanna's computer while I ate.

I read for a moment, finished my oatmeal, put some coffee on to brew, and walked into the living room. I could see a few fires far off on the other side of the bay. Otherwise the landscape was dark except for the electric glow of the city on the left edge of the starless sky. The black limbs of the leafless trees in front of the building stood out like they'd been burned.

I had to get started, so I went back to the computer, opened the browser, and typed in "Pasi Tarkiainen." I didn't find anything new. I tried other searches: "Pasi Tarkiainen" and specific years. I still didn't find anything recent, only information I already knew from the past. Then I combined "Tarkiainen" with other search terms: first his home addresses, then his workplaces. Nothing. I tried combinations of names: "Pasi Tarkiainen Harri Jaatinen." No results. "Pasi Tarkiainen Vasili Gromov." No results. "Pasi Tarkiainen Johanna Lehtinen." A brief news item caught my attention. Another search, this time with Johanna's maiden name: "Pasi Tarkiainen Johanna Merilä."

A cold fist wriggled in my chest, my stomach dropped away to the point of pain, my fingers on the keys started to tremble, and my fingertips were suddenly numb.

It was an article from thirteen years ago.

Johanna was young in the picture, as was Pasi Tarkiainen, of course. He had his right arm around her, and you could see him pulling her closer to him. Johanna's expression was neutral, though there was perhaps a trace of discomfort either from the mere fact of being photographed or because of his overeager squeeze. Tarkiainen's smile was once again broad and radiant, but there wasn't yet that intensity in his eyes that I'd seen in the photo taken several years later.

There was a headline above the picture: ENVIRONMENTALLY EFFICIENT LILLIPUT HOUSES GET THEIR FIRST TWO RESIDENTS.

The article didn't really say anything about Johanna or Pasi Tarkiainen; it was mainly about a new residential development in Kivinokka. A former allotment garden had been converted to housing in the same miniature spirit as garden cottages, with the goal of demonstrating the housing construction of the future. Everything about the neighborhood was twenty years too late—although the houses produced their own energy and were entirely recyclable, sustainable, and nonpolluting, the environment was already so changed by then that the innovations were meaningless. On top of that, the houses were too expensive for an ordinary person to afford, and those who could afford them certainly didn't want to move to Kivinokka. Nowadays the houses were inhabited by anyone brave enough to live in them—the forgotten suburb of Kivinokka had a bad reputation, for a lot of reasons. The area near the bay at Vanhakaupunki was strewn with about a dozen skeletons of high-rises whose builders had run out of money and time before they were completed. But that didn't mean that no one lived there. The people living there didn't mind being off the beaten path.

The nearly decade-and-a-half-old article mentioned that the young couple were a medical student and a journalist, and that they were pleased with their new home. "This place has it all: sustainability, nature, the city, good transit connections." The words were attributed to Pasi Tarkiainen.

I looked at the photo again.

What surprised me the most?

The fact that Johanna had once lived with Pasi Tarkiainen? That she had lived in Kivinokka, just a couple of kilometers from where we lived now? Or that I knew nothing about either of these facts?

I got up, walked to the living room, opened the balcony

door, and went outside. I looked out toward Kivinokka. It was dark, of course, as it almost always was. Here and there fires shone, but otherwise the entire cape was blank darkness but for the angular outlines of the tall black buildings.

Why hadn't Johanna told me about Tarkiainen and the place in Kivinokka? On the other hand, why would she? When we'd met ten years ago and married six months later, it was the beginning of a new life for both of us. So why would we have ever had anything to say about Pasi Tarkiainen or a miniature house they'd lived in thirteen years ago?

It had been a long time since she lived in Kivinokka. When we met she was living in Hakaniemi in a one-bedroom with a kitchen that she'd been in for at least a year and a half. That left another year and a half between the time of the article and her move to Hakaniemi.

Something had happened, and it had happened in a very short time. It may have been nothing more remarkable than the end of young love, though, of course, the discovery of Tarkiainen's DNA at the scenes of the Healer killings and Johanna's disappearance brought to mind other possibilities.

I went back into the kitchen and looked at the picture again, rubbing the cold out of my toes. The photo was cropped so that Johanna Merilä and Pasi Tarkiainen were cut off at the waist and filled the left side of the frame. On the right was a little yellow house with solar panels on the roof, either their house or one of the first to be completed. The caption read: "Johanna Merilä and Pasi Tarkiainen moved to Kivinokka from Kallio."

I looked through Tarkiainen's list of previous addresses. One of them was Pengerkatu 7, in Kallio. I tried an address search under Johanna's name, but all I got was her address on Hämeentie, which I already knew.

I thought for a moment, then picked up my phone.

It was almost seven.

In spite of the time, Elina answered quickly, in a voice that sounded more like someone who'd been awake all night than someone who'd just been awakened.

"Has Johanna been found?" she asked, before I'd finished saying hello.

"No," I said. "Are you still in Helsinki?"

Elina didn't say anything for a moment. Maybe she was checking to see where she was.

"We're still here," she said quietly.

I waited a moment for her to say something more, but she didn't. The silence almost described the way she closed her eyes and hung her head.

"Elina, is everything all right?" I asked.

"No," she said quickly, sharply, then paused a moment and said more cautiously, more softly, "We're not leaving. At least not yet."

"What happened?"

Another silence. I could almost hear her gathering her thoughts and putting them in order. Then she spoke, in a quiet, even tone:

"Ahti was in the basement yesterday getting our things together, and he was bitten by a rat. At first we thought it was nothing, but he woke up last night with a fever, looking yellow, throwing up, and having cramps, and we had to call a doctor. He might have died otherwise. You know there's no point in going to the hospital."

"I know," I said, guessing the end of the story.

"The doctor wouldn't have agreed to come if it weren't for the fact that we could pay in cash. We had the money you gave us, but it wasn't enough. I had to sell our train tickets."

"Did you have enough money then?"

"Enough for the doctor's visit and the antibiotics. And he gave Ahti an injection of something."

"Is Ahti all right?"

"He's sleeping," Elina said, again so quietly that I was almost leaning into the telephone to hear her better. "Or under some kind of sedation. His breathing is rough. Labored, like he can't get enough oxygen."

"Does he have a fever?"

"Not anymore."

"I'm sorry, Elina," I said, trying to make my voice a touch lighter, to pick up the pace. "I'm sure Ahti will recover from this and you'll be able to take your trip. But there's something else I wanted to talk to you about. It has to do with Johanna. And Pasi Tarkiainen."

The phone was completely quiet, with not even the normal background buzz. Elina didn't say anything. I took the phone away from my ear and looked to see if we'd been disconnected. The display said she was still on the line.

"Are you there, Elina?" I asked to make sure.

"Pasi Tarkiainen?" she asked, startled somehow, sounding like she just realized she was still on the telephone.

"Johanna's old boyfriend."

"Yeahhh."

Tense, waiting. That's how she sounded. I asked her in the most patient voice possible: " 'Yeahhh,' meaning that you know him, or 'yeahhh,' meaning that you're waiting for me to ask something else?"

"Yeahhh, I remember Pasi Tarkiainen. Although it was a long time ago. You don't need to worry about it."

The last two sentences came so quickly that at first I didn't understand what she meant.

"No, no, no," I said, when I understood. "That's not why I asked about him."

"Then why?" she asked, surprisingly interested now, positively keen to know.

"I'm not sure yet. Do you remember when Johanna and this Pasi Tarkiainen moved to Kivinokka?"

"Vaguely."

Why was she speaking so quickly now?

"Do you remember anything in particular about that time? Did something happen between them?"

"That's a kind of strange question."

Again the words came quickly, strung together. I sighed.

"I know it is. But do you remember anything?"

"Well, nothing in particular comes to mind. It was a long time ago. Everything was . . . different then."

"Yes, it was," I said, speaking in a consciously slow, clear voice, trying to put the brakes on the speed of her speech. "But Johanna lived there for about a year and a half. Then she moved away."

"This is kind of a weird conversation. Does Pasi have anything to do with your not hearing from Johanna?"

Pasi. I couldn't bring myself to refer to him by his first name. He was Pasi Tarkiainen to me.

"I don't know yet. Elina, try to remember. Was there anything unusual happening, when she moved away from Kivinokka, for instance?"

"I—" she began.

In the background, I could hear a cough coming from deep in the lungs, then two thuds on the wooden floor and an irritated mumble.

"Ahti's awake," Elina said. She sounded positively overjoyed. "Tapani, is it all right if I try to remember and call you later?"

She hung up.

I stood looking at the enlarged image on the computer screen—the lilliputian yellow house bathed in soft spring sunlight, the lush green lawn of the yard, and a man working in the background, his back to the camera, a shovel or rake in his large hands, his shoulders broad, his hair in a ponytail.

11

"YOU COULD HAVE JUST CALLED."

Harri Jaatinen walked around his desk, sat behind it, and looked at me in an uncomfortably fatherly way.

"I was going to call," I said and sat down firmly in a chair. "But I needed to show you some photos and explain some connections between things."

I was aware that I sounded like any number of conspiracy theorists. I held up a hand, although Jaatinen hadn't said anything.

"I'm sure this sounds peculiar. But I did what you suggested: I started with Pasi Tarkiainen." I paused for a second, then two. "And I found my wife. Thirteen years ago."

I explained what had happened, showed Jaatinen the photos, and put several papers in front of him on the desk. He glanced at me before he began to read. There was weariness in his eyes.

The room hummed with the sound of Jaatinen's laptop and the air-conditioning vent in the center of the ceiling. The laptop whirred at a high pitch. Jaatinen read for about five minutes, looked up from the papers, glanced at me—perhaps not as wearily now—looked at the pictures again, and typed something into his computer. Then he leaned back in his chair.

"Good work," he said.

I looked at him in bewilderment.

"That's all?" I said. "Good work?"

"Good work," he said, as if I hadn't understood him. "That's a lot."

"Aren't we going to act? Do something?"

He made a gesture with his left hand that said "Be my guest."

"OK," I said. "What do you think about all this?"

"About all what?"

"About what I've found out."

His voice was as dry and colorless as ever: "What exactly have you found out?"

I raised my eyebrows, sincerely surprised. Hadn't I just explained it to him?

"Pasi Tarkiainen and my wife once lived together. And that bartender was apparently their neighbor from way back. And Gromov, the photographer Johanna was working with, is dead. And all those things must be somehow connected."

"Right," Jaatinen said.

"You agree," I said, leaning forward.

Jaatinen shook his head.

"Only that it all must be somehow connected."

I sighed.

"Can you find out what happened to Gromov?"

Jaatinen glanced at his computer.

"It hasn't been reported yet."

"Are you sure?"

He looked at the computer again, jabbed a finger at the

keyboard a couple of times, and looked at me. Then he spoke, slowly and patiently: "According to this, no one with that name has come in."

"How is that possible?" I asked. "If his employer already knows about it?"

Jaatinen looked at the computer again.

"Anything's possible these days. It could just be that they're busy and won't make a record of it for another week, or another month. But even that wouldn't guarantee anything. Even if the body had come in yesterday and a record was made of it immediately, we might not get any autopsy results until summer. That sort of thing can happen."

I looked at him.

"That wouldn't be much help to Johanna," I said, trying not to seem sarcastic. By the sound of it, I failed.

Jaatinen leaned as far back as possible without putting undue strain on himself or the chair.

"I don't know that it would help her any more if Gromov was on the admission records and the autopsy was under way," he said. "Or if it's any use discussing it. As I said, Johanna Lehtinen did a great service to us—to me—on that case, and that's why I've spent time on you and on this . . . this . . ." he searched for a word for a moment, but couldn't find a suitable one, and half-spoke and half-swallowed the word he did find: "investigation."

I decided to count to ten. I got to six.

"I don't mean to be a prick," I said. "I understand that you're short of staff, flooded with cases, who knows what else. But if Johanna helped you once, now you can help her."

Jaatinen seemed to consider the matter. He looked straight ahead, anyway, and from the look on his face seemed pensive, or just dead tired.

"It's difficult to imagine what I can do," he finally said, "without any detectives."

I looked at him and didn't say anything. He guessed what I was thinking and shook his head.

"Why not?" I said.

He thought for a moment.

"Because."

"Because why?" I said.

"It's a bad situation. Hopeless, in fact. But it's still vaguely under control. If we start using pretend police then that's an admission of defeat on our part."

"I'm not planning to pretend to be the police. At least not outwardly," I said.

Jaatinen looked at me and said without blinking an eye, "OK, suggest something."

I WENT THROUGH THE location signatures on Johanna's phone records that Jaatinen had ordered from the telephone company. I had been right about Jätkäsaari. But it hadn't been the last place Johanna's phone had been turned on.

An hour and forty-five minutes after I'd spoken with her, Johanna's phone had been near a cell phone relay station in the Kamppi area—on the corner of Fredrikinkatu and Urho Kekkosen katu, to be more precise. That was at 10:53 p.m.

I got Jaatinen to have surveillance videos sent to the police servers. The camera was on the corner of the old Sähkötalo building, about ten meters off the ground, and had a wide shot of the entire intersection, so individual people were mere dark shapes that turned pixilated when you enlarged them.

I clicked 10:50 p.m. People came and went by the hundreds. I was sure that in spite of the abundance of people I would be able to spot Johanna in the crowd. The minutes went by. The time record read 10:52, then 10:53, then 10:54. I didn't see Johanna. I clicked back to 10:50 and looked at the three minutes again. And again. I was surprised and disappointed and 100 percent sure that none of the people I saw were Johanna.

I stood up, got some coffee, and sat down in front of the computer again. Jaatinen had brought me to a workroom on the second floor, showed me a computer I could use, and wrote down the password for searching the data. The password got me into the telephone and surveillance camera records and certain identification databanks. The bar at the bottom of the screen said that Jaatinen's computer was linked to this one, and he could see where I was and what I was doing. It also promised to cut off my connections if I went astray.

I was sitting in an open room surrounded by other people tapping on computers. None of them had looked up from their screens, let alone spoken, for the entire hour I'd been sitting there. Maybe we were all doing the same thing: searching and hoping—and, of course, fearing that just one moment of inattention could mean losing that crumb of an answer forever.

I watched the surveillance footage again, focusing on each person's legs. None of them scurried along like Johanna did. She had always laughed at my lazy dawdle. Even though her legs were shorter than mine she walked twice as fast. If she was in the video, I would have seen her. I clicked to the beginning again, leaned back, and watched.

The rain played tricks with the image, soaking the streets and turning the sidewalks shiny, blurring the entire view. At 10:53 the intersection was transformed by the headlights of cars approaching from several directions, combined with the yellow light of the street lamps and the pulsing flash of the signs on the sides of the buildings, into a sparkling bouquet of light, its powerful glow coloring the millions of drops of rain falling from the sky. The result was a landscape that would have made a beautiful painting, but was pretty lousy as evidence.

I sighed and was about to give up, when I realized that I wasn't necessarily looking at the wrong video.

Johanna didn't have to be on foot.

She could just as well have been in a car.

12

I SHOULD BE USED TO LONG SPELLS OF SLIM PRODUCTIVITY, BUT they always seem to take me by surprise. When I'm writing I sometimes sit for hours and hours in front of the computer and only get a few new lines on the screen. Sometimes I just have to content myself with editing old text, a word here, a word there.

I spent an hour enlarging the image and examining it from all angles, writing down partial license numbers and the makes and colors of the cars and searching the drivers' registry—without any luck.

My eyes hurt.

It had been thirty-six hours since Johanna's last phone call.

I closed my eyes. My eyelids felt like stale orange peel. I rubbed them and saw shooting stars flashing from one side of the darkness to the other.

When I lowered my hands, Jaatinen was standing beside me. He looked at the maximum magnification image from the surveillance camera for a moment and then turned to look at me. I didn't say anything.

"Sometimes you don't see it until you stop looking," he said. "You realize something you already knew."

"I suppose."

"I'm going downtown," he said, scanning the screen again. "You can come along, if you want."

I looked at the picture, looked at Jaatinen, and said yes.

Jaatinen's unmarked car was as neutral and metal-gray as the day that was dawning. The sun wasn't exactly shining, but the weather was almost clear, and round-bellied clouds hung low in the sky to remind us that the world still had something other than rain to offer.

Jaatinen's driving was unhurried. He used his turn signal even when no one was there to see it. There was something touching about that, something dignified. I couldn't help but think that he might be one of the last people on earth to obey all laws and statutes. Maybe he read my mind, because he said, "An old habit."

Then he signaled again as we changed lanes to avoid a gap in the asphalt. We reached the Töölö Sports Hall and stopped at the light. The line for the food bank stretched hundreds of meters around the back of the building. I looked at the people in line—expressionless, resigned, their expectations ended. The security guards monitoring the line caught my attention.

There were new security companies springing up all the time, of course, but I didn't remember seeing any guards like these, with their black coveralls and the insignia on their backs. It resembled a large letter A, but not quite. Didn't I remember it from somewhere? Or was I just imagining that I did? I took a few photos of them just in case, both long shots and close-ups of the insignia.

Jaatinen looked at me curiously.

I nodded toward the security guards. He turned to look. I asked if he knew anything about them. He watched them a moment longer and shrugged, then looked at the road ahead again, as if he'd been personally invited to do so.

The light changed and we moved on.

"Sometimes it seems like there's no sense in it," he said. "What are those guys guarding? Making sure people line up in an orderly fashion to get some food that's just going to run out eventually. Who pays them to do that, and why?"

He stopped at another light. The merest hint of a smile crept over his face, surprisingly bright in spite of its faintness and melancholy, lighting up not just his face but the entire car. He glanced at me and said in a gentler tone, "I don't suppose it does any good for me to think about it."

The walls of the Opera House were darkened with rain and damp, its windows covered with plywood and tarps. The square around it, scattered with litter and plain old garbage, was like another world in the still-gray morning light, a world you didn't want to believe was real.

"These things occur to us," I said.

Jaatinen didn't answer. He reached for the gearshift, quickly shifted into neutral, and let up the clutch.

"Can I ask you something?"

The question sounded sincere. I said by all means.

"What did you used to do?"

"I was a poet."

Jaatinen was quiet for a moment. It was comical how the reaction to this simple statement never changed even when the whole world was changing around me. Next he would ask the names of my books and then he would tell me he'd never read them, or heard of them.

"What have you published?" he said.

"*The Most Beautiful Words on Your Lips* was my first collection. Then *A Wind All Winter*, and the last one was *Don't Forget to Remember*."

"I don't think I've ever . . ."

"No need to apologize," I said, smiling. "No one else has, either. I managed to publish three collections before all this started. They sold about two hundred copies each, including library sales. They disappeared a long time ago."

We both watched as an elderly man in a long gray coat tried to help a woman with a scarf on her head cross the street in short, uncertain steps before the light changed. The curb was too high for her, and the man didn't have the strength to lift her onto the sidewalk. Somehow they leaned on each other and, one step at a time, hauled each other over it. A bus rushed by with its horn blaring, its side mirror missing the old man's head by mere centimeters.

"My daughter's in Norway," Jaatinen said, taking me by surprise. "She's been there four years now, ever since Irina, her mother—my wife—died. A drug runner ran her down with his SUV as she was riding her bike to work."

I glanced at him. He was still watching the old couple.

"The driver got a year and a half probation. I got single parenthood. Which didn't go well, of course, since I'm always at work. I have to be at work—school and day care cost so much. When my daughter's godparents suggested that she come stay with them in Norway, I said yes. I don't know if that was the right thing to do. And I don't know what else I could do. As long as I keep earning, we can afford for her to live there."

Hotels loomed on the right, the flags in their courtyards fluttering in the morning wind. They were full. Who would have guessed that Finland would benefit from people losing their homes in the south?

I didn't know what to say to Jaatinen. It didn't matter, since he continued his story without waiting for me to comment.

"To send her to Norway, I had to sell my little house in Korso. I was lucky I managed to sell it at all. Several young families bought it, some kind of shared living arrangement, for safety. They bought it for half of what I paid for it, but for some reason the debt I had left didn't trouble me."

"Where do you live now?" I asked, for something to say.

"In Pasila."

"You must have a short commute to work, then."

"From the basement to the fourth floor."

He smiled again, but his eyes weren't along for the smile.

We passed Parliament House, which was surrounded by security barriers with twenty-four-hour floodlights on top. Their light looked feverish in the metallic gray of the morning.

"I meant what I said before," Jaatinen said.

"What was that?" I asked.

"That I keep trying because I'm a cop. I'm not one of these unemployed cops working as a security guard, playing soldier. That's why I didn't answer right away when you asked about those guards with the "A" logo at the Sports Hall. It's a new security company, as you probably guessed. The fastest growing one. Aggressive. Feared, in fact."

He switched on his turn signal and changed lanes.

"These security companies are all the same, if you ask me. Most of the guards aren't cut out for protecting the public and keeping order. More cut out for something entirely the opposite, in fact. We know of one security company that actually robs people and businesses instead of protecting them."

Jaatinen dropped me off at the corner by the Forum. I got out of the car, and he eased back into traffic—with his signal on, of course. I dug my phone out of my pocket, looked at the photos I'd taken, clipped an image of the "A" logo and did an image search on it.

The company was called A-Secure. There was no specific information on it, no street address. The phone numbers online didn't return any names when I searched for them. I looked at the logo again but still didn't know what it was I expected it to tell me.

I crossed the street and headed toward Urho Kekkosen katu, for something to do.

13

"Do you think we'll ever move again?" Johanna asked one night two or three weeks ago just as she was about to fall asleep.

I put down the book I was reading. Johanna pressed against me, the blanket rustling, and laid her head partly on the pillow, partly against my neck. The soft light of the reading lamp shone on the golden yellow of her skin. At a glance, her delicate arm lying across my stomach on the black-and-white blanket resembled a doll's.

"Why do you ask that?"

"I was just thinking," she said, and I could almost feel her lips against my neck as she spoke.

"Would you like to move?" I asked.

"I guess not."

"What about just for pretend?"

"Maybe just for pretend."

"Where would you move to, just for pretend?"

"That's the thing," she said, raising her head from the pillow and wrapping herself halfway around me. "There's no place I'd like to move to, except for pretend."

She braced herself on an elbow.

"I've been going around Helsinki the past few days working on this story. I went to a lot of places I haven't seen for a long time, and I kept getting a really sad, wistful feeling."

"A lot of places have changed quite a bit the past few years. Even right around here."

"I guess so," she said. "But when you see places where you used to live and you remember what they used to be like and all the things you did there and all the people you knew . . . friends, family, people like that."

Thinking about this conversation later, I knew, of course, that I should have asked her where she had gone, why she went there, what she found there. But it was an ordinary evening and we were just lying in bed talking like we always did, like we always would.

"It also made me wonder," she said, "whether people could have done something else, something more. Done things differently. But at the same time I know that they couldn't."

Everything she said that night had an insidious underlying meaning now: Pasi Tarkiainen. He was the snake that slipped into my thoughts through the smallest opening and poisoned all my memories. I shook him forcefully from my mind and saw Johanna before me again.

She raised her head and looked into my eyes from so close that it was difficult to clearly see the flecks of color in her irises, her hard, black pupils, or the expression behind their moist surface.

"On the one hand, we've got so much," she said. "But at the same time, so much is already lost."

I took her hand. She answered with a gentle squeeze.

"If I understand you correctly, we're not moving."

A dark shadow crossed her gaze quick as lightning, then vanished. She smiled.

"Let's not," she said quietly.

She heaved herself up, putting her hand on the pillow beside my ear and bending over to kiss me with warm, soft lips.

"Let's not," she said again.

A PIT HAD APPEARED at the intersection of Urho Kekkosen katu and Fredrikinkatu. Some men were crowded around it, and an excavator stood with its shovel raised on one side of it. Trucks from the electricity and water departments were lined up in front of the pit facing Fredrikinkatu as if waiting to drive into it. Traffic was driving up over the curb to get around it.

I stood on the corner, pulled my scarf tighter around my neck, zipped my parka all the way up, readjusted my stocking cap, and carefully pushed the cuffs of my gloves into the ends of my sleeves. When one of the workers from the water department, a red-faced man in winter coveralls, walked by me, I asked him what had happened. As you can see, he said, there's been a cave-in. I couldn't get any more information out of him, but then there was no reason I should.

I walked around the intersection and looked first at Temppeliaukio Church, then at Malminkatu, Fredrikinkatu, Urho Kekkosen katu, and then at the church again. Now and then I looked at the pit in the middle of the intersection. Since there was nothing in any direction to see but the pit, and since the wind seemed to be growing teeth, I gave up and headed toward Töölö, to Ahti and Elina's house.

When is it time to admit that you don't know someone as well as you thought you did a moment before?

I tried to gather the facts in my mind as neutrally as I could, to filter truth from imagination. I tried to separate my worst fears from what I could see with my own eyes to be true. It wasn't easy, but it was for the woman I love. No matter how I tried, I couldn't remember Johanna ever mentioning anything about Tarkiainen or ever saying a word about the house in Kivinokka. But then I couldn't think of a reason why she would, either. She had no reason to. Who could have predicted that Tarkiainen's and Johanna's paths would cross again?

I crossed the bridge between Eteläisen and Pohjoisen Rautatiekatu and looked down. Cars driven under the bridge and abandoned there now formed a row of small dwellings. The narrow passage under the bridge had been growing into its own neighborhood for several years. I could see smoke and steam rising, and smell grilling meat, gasoline—and moonshine, of course. The shouts of children could be heard here and there, playing a game, or shouting for other reasons.

I looked at my watch. It was almost ten. The minutes and hours seemed to pass more quickly as time went by. I reached Arkadiankatu, took out my telephone, and tried to call Johanna, with the same results as before. How many times would I try to call her? How many times would I listen to the toneless recorded voice of the woman telling me again and again what I knew only too well? I didn't know. Maybe events had to be repeated until the repetition produced results, or until it was useless to try.

A tram full of people coming from downtown rattled past a couple of meters from me. The passengers standing near the door had their coats pressed up against the windows. Countless people on their way to work, on an ordinary day, getting on with their lives. The tram thudded to a stop and I continued walking, the cold wind, the smell of burned meat, and the angry stench of ethanol elbowing me in the back as I went.

I arrived at Ahti and Elina's building, pressed the buzzer, and waited a moment. The camera moved under its hood like an insect's antenna as it made its little circuit of the entrance. When it had assured itself that I wasn't a threat, it stopped, the lock on the door opened, and I went inside. Although the elevator was waiting in the lobby, I took the stairs. My footsteps on the stone staircase rang like drumbeats in the quiet building.

The smell of a sickroom hit me as soon as I walked into the apartment. Elina's face was small and pale in the electric light of the entryway. She nodded in greeting, turned, and walked into the living room. I pulled the door closed behind me, took off my coat and shoes, and followed her, pausing at the door to the bedroom to hear Ahti's snores and see his feet under the covers at the foot of the bed. I was about to take a step into the room but decided against it.

Elina sat on the sofa with her feet tucked under her, her long hair lying all in a clump on her left shoulder. Once again the soft light gave the room a feeling that it had been forcibly frozen in time, an overly homey feeling. That was what bothered me about it. It felt like a fantasy, an attempt to return to the past.

I sat down in an imposing armchair that was covered in rough black fabric. It instantly warmed and relaxed my tired frame. I became aware of how exhausted and hungry I was, and of how little I felt like eating anything or making myself comfortable.

"Luckily he's sleeping again," Elina said. "Since he's not really awake when he's awake. He was so mixed up when he was talking just a while ago that it scared me."

"I'm sorry Ahti's sick. I'm sorry your trip's been delayed."

Elina gave a yelping laugh, but there was no joy in it. She took a breath, exhaled quickly, and lifted her left hand to her forehead, like she'd just remembered something.

"I'm sorry. I'm a little tired," she said. "Tired of everything."

"That's all right," I said. "It's just a temporary setback. We'll think of something."

Elina didn't say anything but glanced toward the bedroom and looked for a moment like she was listening very carefully to something that my ears, at least, couldn't hear.

"Elina, we have to talk," I said.

She looked at me again, her gaze sharper, colder.

"About Pasi Tarkiainen?"

I nodded. About Pasi Tarkiainen.

"What does he have to do with anything?" Elina asked. "With finding Johanna or anything else? It was all years ago, fifteen years or so. What does it matter?"

"I have a theory that Tarkiainen does have something to do with it."

She stroked her hair with one hand and tugged at the hem of her sweater with the other.

"Johanna and Pasi lived together in Kivinokka, didn't they?" I asked.

Elina nodded—not right away, but she nodded nevertheless.

"I find it hard to believe that digging up the past will help you find Johanna," Elina said. "But go ahead. Do what you like."

She sighed and tucked her feet tighter beneath her.

"We lived a different kind of life then," she said. "We were young and naive. Students. We did everything together. Some things we shouldn't have done."

"Like what?"

"Like things Pasi thought of." Elina glanced at me, saw the expression on my face, and laughed again. This laugh was noticeably more genuine than the previous one. "It's not what you're thinking. Pasi Tarkiainen was a radical environmentalist back then. That's the kind of thing I'm talking about."

"I see," I said, and realized I was blushing.

"You're jealous," Elina said.

I nodded reluctantly, feeling heat in my cheeks.

"This all happened a long time ago. I'm sure you have a past, too."

"Of course I do," I said, feeling the heat spread to my neck and wanting to change the subject. "What were these ideas of Pasi's?"

"He was a hard-line conservationist. He had contacts with the kinds of groups that were starting to shoot company owners and politicians—anyone who had caused environmental destruction or hadn't done enough to slow it down. It was the black-and-white thinking of youth: if you're not with us, you're against us, and you don't deserve to live. Johanna and I waved that flag, too. In secret, that is. But we believed it."

"I didn't know you were so radical," I said. "I mean, I knew that Johanna was an activist, but I didn't know that she'd been living with a terrorist."

Elina looked for a moment like she was trying to remember how things really were. The coolness was disappearing from her gaze little by little.

"Pasi wasn't a terrorist. A passionate person, even an obsessive person, yes, but he wasn't a bad person. He hasn't done anything wrong, has he?"

I thought of the murdered families and the evidence that Tarkiainen was at the scenes of those crimes. I shrugged and let the question pass.

"Why is it so hard for you to talk about?" I asked.

Elina nodded toward the bedroom.

"Ahti doesn't really understand," she said, then added faintly, almost involuntarily, "for a lot of reasons."

I looked at her.

"Haven't the two of you ever talked about it?" I asked.

She looked surprised and offended for a moment, then just surprised.

"Why would we? You and Johanna didn't."

The truth stung.

"No, we didn't. I guess there wasn't any reason to."

"You were happy as long as you thought you knew everything you needed to know," Elina said. "And now that you know that there were things you didn't know, you feel bad. You've got to make up your mind about how much you really want to know. Even about your own wife."

There was something in her voice that I'd never noticed before. The coolness had returned, and with it something hard, even bitter.

"Tell me more about Pasi Tarkiainen," I said.

"Why?"

I looked her in the eye.

"You haven't told me everything."

She let out a puff of air and rolled her eyes. But she was a bad actor. Even she knew it.

"You're not going to find Johanna by digging up things that happened a hundred years ago."

"You haven't told me everything," I said again. "Ahti's asleep. You can tell me."

She glanced toward the bedroom again. We listened to the silence for a moment. I could hear Ahti snoring.

"This is important, Elina," I said. "Johanna has been missing for a day and a half. I don't even want to think about any other possibility but finding her alive, unhurt. I need all the help I can get. It's not easy to ask, but I have to. I have to find Johanna."

Elina pulled her legs up even closer, brushed the hair from her face with a few quick movements of her hand, and looked straight ahead for a moment. Then she looked at me again, her head bowed a little, and said, as if she were surrendering something:

"I adored Pasi Tarkiainen."

She was still looking at me, perhaps waiting for some reaction. Then she continued: "I don't know how to explain it now, but I adored him. And, of course, I wished that he adored me in the same way. But it was Johanna he wanted. I can admit it now—now that it's been so many years. I was in love with Pasi, and I was dying of jealousy when I saw how happy they were together."

I wasn't surprised.

"Did you tell Johanna about it?"

"No," Elina said quickly, shaking her head. "I didn't even tell Pasi about it. I just tried to make him notice me. And then when I heard that they weren't really that happy, at first I was pleased, but then I was just sorry, thinking, What kind of person am I that I'm happy when my friend's partner is revealed to be something other than he seems, when I learn that she's not happy?"

"What happened?"

"I don't really know," Elina said, and she sounded sincere. "All Johanna told me was that Pasi wasn't the man she had thought he was. Sometimes if I'd had a glass of wine, or two or three, I would ask about it, but somehow we just didn't talk about it, even though we talked about everything together. Pasi just disappeared from our lives, and we forgot about him.

Then Ahti came along, and you, and everything that had to do with Pasi had vanished."

She smiled an entirely joyless smile.

"I've never talked with anyone about this. Not even Johanna. It seems like a different world now. It feels like ages ago, like I'm a different person now, and so is everyone else."

I didn't say anything.

"Johanna's my best friend," she said. "The best friend I've ever had or ever will have. I love Ahti. Ahti's my husband. But Johanna's my friend."

I still didn't say anything. I leaned my elbows on my knees and looked at her, her brown eyes still shining with the anger of a moment earlier, the shadows on her face. All the coldness and hardness had gone out of her face, but something dark still lingered.

"And now here we are," she said in the same resigned tone that she'd begun with. "Last night I started thinking, Why in the world are we going north? That won't solve anything. Nothing. We'll have even less there than we have here. I want you to find Johanna, so we can be together again. You and Johanna and Ahti are all the family I have left. My parents both died of the flu four years ago, my big sister is somewhere in America, and she's not coming back. I was sitting beside Ahti last night thinking that no matter what comes, we don't need to leave here. We shouldn't."

She lifted her head. A delicate smile lit up her face, its warmth slowly rising to her eyes.

"Let's stick together and live as long as we can, as long as we're able to," she said softly, then added faintly, troubled, "let's do the best we can under the circumstances."

Ahti didn't awaken even when I was purposefully noisy putting on my coat and shoes at the door. I would have liked to talk to him, but Elina felt we should let him keep snoring. I asked her to call me if she remembered something, anything at all, about Pasi Tarkiainen.

I tried to show her Tarkiainen's picture, told her that he'd lived on Museokatu, just a little way from here, a few years before she and Ahti had moved into the neighborhood. But she didn't want to look at a photo of her former infatuation or think about how close he had once lived to where she was now.

I got a few names from her, people from her student days and even later. One of them was someone I knew: Laura Vuola, Ph.D. Her name brought to mind things that I'd imagined were settled and forgotten. It almost made me doubt my sanity: the beginnings of this whole tangled web had been so close to me, and I was blissfully ignorant of all of it. I didn't mention it to Elina.

I thanked her and embraced her longer than I meant to, pulling away when I realized what I was doing.

14

THE INCIPIENT CLARITY OF THE MORNING HAD GROWN DAMP WHILE I was indoors, with intermittent wind and clouds covering a sky that promised rain and darkened the world in the meantime.

I knew why I had held on to Elina for so long. I missed Johanna physically, too: her dense warmth, her distinct wool and honey scent, the feel of her small frame beside me, close to me, the way her hand fit into mine. We were affectionate with each other, all the time. That's why missing her came so quickly, so deeply, so sharply. I looked up, sighed, pushed all my thoughts of Johanna to the back of my mind, and let only one thought come front and center: I'll find you.

I walked toward Museokatu, intending to visit that same tavern. I didn't know if it would be open, but I remembered that it used to be even in the mornings. Thirsty artists and those who thought they were artists used to gather there to level out the holes and hummocks left by the night.

I descended the stone stairs from Temppelikatu to Oksasenkatu. I couldn't begin to count the times I'd walked down those stairs before. When I got to the bottom I looked behind me at the sturdy stones, the bolted steel door of the weightlifters' gym halfway up, the large moss-covered rocks resting against the railing.

I stopped at the corner of Tunturikatu. Farther down the street was the flea market. The entire space was filled with stuff. Some of it had even been carried out to the sidewalk. It was difficult to imagine why anyone would go there. What would they have bought? Clothes, which everyone had too much of already? Dishes, when there wasn't enough food? Electronics that gave only a moment's pleasure even when they were new? Books and records that no one had any time to read or listen to anymore?

A sculpture of two bears facing each other watched over the intersection of Museokatu and Oksasenkatu. Two teddy bears, really—they were so small. Their handsome gray coats of stone were covered in a green fuzz of mold.

The tavern door was open. I could hear music coming from inside. I walked up the steps, smelling the same mixture of sweat and urine that I remembered, now masked by the smell of disinfectant. Nobody was behind the bar. Some customers sat at a few tables on the left side of the room, each one alone, fiddling with their phones or staring into space.

I stood there, wondering how to proceed if I encountered the bartender with the ponytail. I waited a couple of minutes. The door to the back room opened, and a moment later a heavyset bodybuilding type came out with a clinking brown cardboard box in his arms. He put the box down on the counter and looked at me questioningly.

I ordered coffee.

He turned without nodding or saying a word, took a cup down from the upper shelf, and filled it from the coffeepot, which looked like it had been sitting there since the place opened. Or since it closed. He plunked the mug on the bar in front of me and stood waiting. He was young, maybe twenty, and seemed composed entirely of large individual and incompatible masses of muscle. His blue eyes were squeezed between his brow ridge and his cheekbones, and you could see the squeeze in his gaze.

"Are you gonna pay?" he said.

"How much would I pay if I did pay?" I answered.

He turned around slowly and pointed at the menu on the wall in a pose that gave me a good look at his arm.

"It starts with a K. Then an A. Then H and V, and one little I. That spells KAHVI. And that number after it tells you how much it costs."

I dug a coin out of my pocket and tossed it on the counter. He didn't put it in the cash register, but instead dropped it into the glass mug next to it. Then he started taking bottles out of the cardboard box. After a while he noticed me watching him. He straightened up and turned toward me.

"Don't tell me," he said. "You forgot to ask for milk."

The air conditioner hummed. I didn't say anything.

"Sugar?"

He sighed and put his hands on his hips.

"So you're just a mad starer, are you?" he said. "OK. Drink your coffee and get outta here."

"I'm not a mad starer. But I'd be happy to drink my coffee and get out of here if you'll tell me where I can find the bartender who was working here last night. Big guy with a ponytail. Is he working today?"

He took his hands off his hips and folded his arms across his chest, screwed up his lips, and looked at me like I was cluttering up his decor.

"I think you better finish your coffee—"

"And get outta here. I understand. Is he coming in to work today? Or do you have the guy's phone number?"

"What do you want with his phone number?"

I looked at him for a moment.

"I thought I might call him," I offered.

"Why?"

"Why do people usually call each other? Maybe I'm a friend of his who lost his number."

"You don't look like a friend of his."

I looked at him again.

"What do you think a friend looks like?" I asked. "Do his friends look different than friends usually do? How can you tell if somebody's a friend of his?"

His eyebrows and cheekbones seemed to be squeezing his eyes right out of his head now.

"What kinda clown are you?"

"I'm not a clown."

"You are a clown 'cause I said you're a clown."

I took a breath. My body ached with exhaustion and frustration. I realized that there was no point in bantering with him—it would only make my task harder if I got into an argument—but I couldn't stop myself.

"That's not how it works," I said. "Things aren't what you say they are just because you say it. Some small children believe that, but you're an adult—or you look like one, anyway."

"Are you trying to fuck with me?"

"No, I'm just looking for the bartender that was here yesterday, the guy with the ponytail."

He took a couple of steps toward me, leaving just the half-meter-wide glass-covered counter between us. I glanced to my left, toward the barroom. The music apparently blotted out our little exchange because the eyes of the clientele stayed glued to their telephones, the tabletops, and the empty air.

"Get lost," he said.

"Or else what?" I asked, suddenly completely tired of the conversation and every other difficulty I was encountering. "What's the guy's name?"

"Go fuck yourself."

"OK. And where does this Go Fuck Yourself live?"

"Up your ass."

"You must've skipped biology. Along with all your other classes, I'll bet. What classes did you go to?"

"The classes on how to cut morons like you to pieces."

"Oh, do they still teach that? I was under the impression that they'd practically discontinued that kind of instruction. It's good to hear that children are still being properly educated."

He leaned over the counter and raised his hand. A retractable baton clicked out to its full length. I backed away. Thrown out of the same bar for the second time in twenty-four hours, I backed up all the way to the door and stopped.

"Tell him hello from me," I said.

He came around the bar after me. I was already in the street and walked quickly toward the center of town, satisfied with my visit. It was a sure thing that word would get around and eventually reach the right ears. If I couldn't find Tarkiainen, I'd let him find me.

15

THE MOUSE-GRAY, DRIZZLY DAY WAS HALF OVER WHEN I STEPPED off a tram full of damp clothes, violent coughs, and worried looks at the stop in front of Stockmann department store. Downtown Helsinki was doing its best to remind us that tomorrow was Christmas Eve. Here and there a lone string of Christmas lights twinkled desperately, looking in their feeble glimmer like they missed not just their finer days but also their lost comrades.

A few drops of rain fell on my face, all the colder for their paucity. I wiped them away, slipped into the flow of people, and didn't notice until I was halfway across the street that I was walking into the middle of traffic. I heard a choir singing "Silent Night" from somewhere up ahead.

There was a large decorated spruce tree at Three Smiths Square. Its red and yellow lights glowed in the drizzle like thousands of little traffic signals escaped from their poles. Next to the tree an armored police car was parked. There were a lot of police on foot, too, as well as private security guards. The security guards walked in pairs wearing black or gray coveralls, a few of them crossing in front of traffic, and as many on the sidewalks as there were Christmas shoppers. I counted six security guards under the clock in front of the entrance to Stockmann. And there were more inside the store, of course, in plain clothes.

Charities collecting donations lined the square. Everybody could use some cash. The recipients were mostly people in Finland and nearby countries: schools, hospitals, children's services. The Salvation Army's traditional kettle stood in the middle of the square. A Salvation Army choir stood around it—four women and three men singing "Silent Night."

I dug a bill out of my pocket and dropped it in the kettle. I thought about how I was eating up our savings—the money I'd spent over the past day and a half was more than I'd spent in the previous six months put together. The savings were supposed to be for emergencies. If Johanna's disappearance wasn't an emergency, then what would be? I dropped another few coins into the pot and continued east on Aleksanterinkatu.

I passed windows that promised discounts of up to 95 percent. The jewelry stores were advertising brand-name watches at prices that would have caused a stampede a year earlier, but now the gold and platinum timepieces sat in their glass cases measuring a time that no longer existed.

The fast food places had all closed. The shoe stores and clothing stores were toughing it out with the help of Christmas shoppers. The tavern on the corner of Mikonkatu and Aleksanterinkatu had a sign advertising cheap beer and lunch, with lunch crossed out.

I turned left on Mikonkatu, continued right on Yliopistonkatu, and found myself in the middle of a fight.

The large, broad-shouldered, bald man who looked like a native Finn was wearing a short leather jacket. He seemed an overwhelming opponent for the other man, a slim young Asian in a hooded sweatshirt who was little more than a boy. The bald man was trying to get the younger one in front of his hefty fists, and the young one was dodging them nimbly. After evading a few right jabs, he let his left foot do the talking.

The kick surprised everyone, but especially the bald fellow. The thump and the crunch of the bone in his nose could be heard from meters away. He staggered and tried one last punch, throwing all his weight behind it. The young man dodged him again and answered with a high, quick right-legged kick that struck the bald one somewhere in the vicinity of his ear and looked and sounded like it hurt.

The older man's arms dropped to his sides, and the young man moved in front of him. He busted the older man's lip with two swift smacks, like opening a packet of ketchup, and ended with three blows to his chin, which seemed to give way under the lightning-quick punches.

The man fell to the ground, first onto his ass, where he sat with empty eyes and a bloody face, then onto his side on the asphalt as if lying down in bed for a nap. The younger man turned and walked to where a friend was standing, took his coat from him, and looked back. There was no triumph on his face, or any feeling at all. The whole episode had lasted less than thirty seconds. The two men walked off toward the railway station.

I continued on to the university. The small plaza in front of Porthania Hall was silent and deserted, which wasn't surprising considering it was Christmas Eve and drizzling. The revolving door was still revolving, however, and I went inside.

I had called Laura, who had, of course, been surprised that I got in touch with her. Under the polite distance in her voice there had been a touch of alarm, perhaps even fear. I didn't talk for long. As soon as she said that she was at her office at the university, and that there was a porter and a few professors working in spite of the holidays, for the physical and spiritual support of the students and for sheer scholarly tenaciousness, I said I wanted to come see her. All right, she said, after a moment's silence.

Laura Vuola, the love of my life—twenty years ago.

I remembered clearly the first time we met, at the political science department Christmas party, on the fifth floor of the New Student House, Laura in her long-necked, wine-red sweater and dark lipstick, my amazement and triumph when she agreed to leave with me, the walk through downtown in the snow to her apartment—Laivurinkatu 37.

And I remembered the times I walked back to my place in Töölö after one of our arguments, the desolate, black winter wind tearing through the city. Laura had seen the truth quickly: I wasn't ambitious, determined, or career oriented at all. If someone had told me that opposites attract, I would have told them the story of Laura and me.

I walked through the metal detector in the lobby, taking off my belt and shoes, like I did nearly everywhere I went, it seemed. A red-eyed woman handed them back to me and flicked her bleached hair away from her face without saying a word, then sat down in her chair and went back to playing a first-person shooter on her phone.

I climbed the spiral staircase past the cafeteria where, in another life long ago, I used to sit and talk, sometimes for hours, over a single cup of coffee.

The glass doors on the third floor were locked. There was a buzzer on the wall with a sign over it that said JUST PRESS IT ONCE—WE CAN HEAR YOU. I pressed the button once and hoped I would be heard.

16

SOMETIMES YOU DO REMEMBER CORRECTLY.

Laura's hair was still long, dark, and slightly curly, parted evenly in the middle and combed to either side of her fair, almost pale face. Her high cheekbones and slightly fuller than ordinary lips gave her face a sort of Mediterranean look, as did her brown eyes and long dark eyelashes.

Laura still seemed to be a proud riddle. I remembered very well how I used to want to solve that riddle.

"I don't need to tell you that this is quite a surprise."

Her voice was still low, echoing through the quiet stairwell.

"I'm not really sure what you need to tell me."

"Should we start arguing right here at the door, or would you like to come in first?"

I had to smile.

"I didn't come to argue," I said. "Thanks for agreeing to meet me."

Now Laura smiled. Her smile was wary, probing.

"Anyway, nice to see you."

She showed me in and made sure the door was locked behind me.

She was dressed in the same timeless way that she used to be: an elegant gray sweater with a copious collar whose numerous folds hung in layers down her front, a long tweed skirt, and light brown high-heeled leather boots, which made her taller than I was.

She had an office at the end of the hall, its walls lined with shelves full of books, journals, and stacks of paper. There was a narrow window on one side that showed a slice of the wall of the building opposite. It was hard to believe that even an ambitious professor of literature could get anything out of a view like that.

Laura sat at her desk, her chair yielding to her as if taking her in its arms. I backed into the other seat in the office, an upholstered sofa that was the shortest I'd ever seen. Although we were as far away from each other as the office space allowed, the distance between us was a meter and a half, at most. She looked at me, her brown eyes open and curious.

"You're a poet now."

I didn't answer right away. I looked at her and remembered how easy it was to just sit and stare at her, waiting for her to reveal the smallest opening into her secrets. Maybe there never were any secrets, except in my imagination.

"And you're a literature professor. Just as you should be. You were always a wee bit more ambitious than I was."

"You haven't lost your sarcasm," Laura said.

There didn't seem to be any help for it. Her quick answers still left me at a loss. And there was something else. Looking at my long-lost love, I understood how much I yearned for my present one.

"I'm sorry," I said. "I meant that I'm happy for you. Honest."

"Thanks."

She looked away.

"The youngest professor of literature they've ever had," she said. "And a woman. It wasn't easy."

"I'm sure it wasn't," I said.

"You've got to have strong elbows," she said. "But I'm sure you remember that. Strong, sharp elbows. Literally."

I showed with my smile that I did remember, not letting my face show even a trace of how painfully. I had already noticed the diamond ring on her left hand. I nodded toward it.

"You're married."

She didn't look at the ring.

"Samuli died a year ago. Tuberculosis."

"I'm sorry."

"We have a son, Otto. He's thirteen."

"That's wonderful. Congratulations."

Were all meetings after a break of twenty years this tense, this full of traps and land mines? Laura looked at me again.

"So you really became a poet," she said.

"After some setbacks."

"Unfortunately, I haven't . . ."

"That's all right," I said. "Neither has anyone else. They only came out with a couple hundred copies. The kinds of books that have a small audience. And it was before all this."

We sat quietly for a moment.

"Have you ever thought about what it would have been like if things had been different?" she asked, taking me completely by surprise. I shrugged.

"Different how?" I asked. "Between us, or in general?"

"In all ways," she said. "Completely different. If everything had had a happy ending."

I looked at her. Was I understanding her correctly? Was

she doubting the choices she'd made? If she was, then this was a Laura I'd never met before.

"I don't know," I said. "Maybe this is the happy ending."

"Maybe it is."

"Laura," I said when I saw that she was sinking deep into her thoughts, "I have something important I want to talk with you about. My wife has disappeared. You may be able to help me. I'm looking for a man named Pasi Tarkiainen."

A pair of furrows appeared on her brow and her full lips turned down. It was an expression I remembered.

"I don't quite understand," she said, as I had expected she would. "Has your wife gone somewhere with Tarkiainen?"

I shook my head and realized that I was doing it much more patiently than I would have twenty years earlier.

"If she did, she didn't go voluntarily. You remember him, then?"

"Who doesn't?" she said, and immediately sounded uneasy. "Everybody remembers Pasi Tarkiainen. He was a charismatic young student and environmental activist. Extremely opinionated and, I have to admit, extremely attractive. In retrospect, he was right about the seriousness of the situation, but his methods . . ."

"I've heard about his methods," I said. "And they may have to do with why my wife got lost looking for him."

"Has Pasi, I mean Tarkiainen," she looked me in the eye, searching for the right words, "has he done something?"

"Maybe. I don't know. To be honest, Laura, I'm at my wit's end. I'm desperate. The only thing I know for sure is that my wife has disappeared. Everything else is speculation. I'm hunting for anything that's even remotely connected."

"How long has she been missing?"

I instinctively looked at my watch before I knew what I was doing and stopped myself.

"A day and a half. Almost two."

"Have you told the poli—"

"Laura," I interrupted, so quickly and bluntly that I startled even myself. "It was the police who gave me the tip about Tarkiainen. Since I have nothing else to look for, I'm looking for him. The police won't do anything. They can't do anything."

My voice had risen, its tone turned sharp and hard. I realized that. The look on Laura's face was familiar from the past.

"Sorry," I said.

"That's all right. It's almost like old times. Now it's my turn to raise my voice."

We were quiet for a moment, then she started to smile. So did I. Tense. Traps and land mines.

"It's good that we postponed arguing until we were comfortably seated, at least," she said.

I started to laugh, for the first time in a long time. The laugh spread through my body like the warmth of a touch. It felt good.

"Should I start accusing you of living in a fantasy world, of being ineffectual and directionless?" Laura said.

"Go ahead." I laughed. "And I'll tell you how calculating you are, a backstabber, a social climber."

Laura stopped laughing, but her smile still spilled all the way to her big brown eyes.

"I liked you," she said. "In spite of everything."

I looked at her.

"I liked you, too."

She was still smiling.

"Maybe there's no point in wondering if things could have been different, on a big scale or a small scale," she said.

"Things are what they are," I said.

There was warmth in her eyes now, the kind I had wished for twenty years ago.

"The two of you are happy."

"Extremely happy," I agreed.

"I'm happy for you."

"Thanks."

When I said nothing more, she took a breath.

"So. Tarkiainen."

She talked about Tarkiainen, and I listened without interrupting. The chronology of the story was familiar from what Elina had told me: first idealistic activism, then conversion to single-minded radicalism, and finally disillusioned withdrawal. Where to, she didn't know, and I couldn't tell her.

Laura had got to know Tarkiainen at the end of her student days when information about the severity of climate change temporarily united people and laid the framework for many fine and well-meaning organizations, associations, and political parties.

But now we know that unity was only momentary, Laura concluded, and I noticed her voice speeding up a little. That fight was won by big business—in other words, a few thousand people who were already superrich, who once again masked their own interests in the mantle of economic growth for the common good. The return to the old ways was echoed by the desire of a populace tired of momentary scarcity, of consuming less, to live like they had before: self-absorbed, greedy, and irresponsible—the way they'd always been taught to live.

So the vision of the long-term common good was once again defeated by ever larger houses, newer cars, wider television screens, homes renovated once a year, stereos, radios, toasters, mixers, filters, browsers, and, of course, new wardrobes every week or so. And you had to get everything cheaper than it had ever been before. Which sped up the cycle of destruction exponentially.

I didn't want to interrupt her to say that she was oversimplifying, exaggerating. I knew she knew it herself. Maybe she just needed to vent her frustration to someone, so why not me? I also selfishly hoped that she would soon get to the reason I came.

She did stop to take a breath and returned to Tarkiainen, the charismatic young man she remembered from fifteen years earlier. She talked about joining Tarkiainen to found an activist group for young academics. The original purpose of the group was to form a new people's movement independent of politics, but Tarkiainen had other ideas right away. That was when Tarkiainen started learning about fringe groups practicing direct action. She thought it was possible that he had participated in some of their attacks. In any case, he took up a radical, militant environmentalism—if you're even the slightest bit involved in consumption or nonecological activity, then you're 100 percent against us—and he quickly dropped out of the group Laura belonged to.

It sent a shiver down my spine when she mentioned Tarkiainen's girlfriend: a young, small, attractive woman with blue-green eyes, whose name she couldn't remember at the moment.

"Johanna," I said quietly.

A flash of memory and recognition shone in her eyes, and she nodded.

"That's it," she said. "How did you—"

"Johanna's my wife."

The room fell silent. So silent that I could hear shreds of hallway conversation in an entirely different part of the building. The Laura I once knew wouldn't have felt comfortable going so long without speaking, but this Laura sat calmly in her chair, sunk once again in thought.

"What do you remember about Johanna?" I asked.

She shrugged.

"She was in the group for a while. I remember I thought that she was there sort of reluctantly. Maybe she realized before the rest of us did that Tarkiainen had changed his outlook."

"So why did she stay, then?"

Now Laura looked me in the eye, raised her eyebrows, and snorted with amusement.

"Maybe she hoped she could change him, straighten him out, influence his thinking. People will believe all kinds of things. Even smart people."

There was obviously no point in continuing in this vein. And in spite of the fact that I felt conflicted and uncomfortable asking my former girlfriend about my present wife, I continued: "What kind of relationship do you think they had—Johanna and Tarkiainen?"

"That was fifteen years ago," she said, shaking her head. "And I couldn't have told you even back then. But I think they had a relationship that began with a shared goal, and then one of them changed his goal to something the other couldn't care less about. That sort of thing happens. I think when your wife, I mean Johanna, finally noticed that Tarkiainen had risen to another sphere of his own, she tried to get into it as long as she could. Just like I would have done. Even though that was a risky thing to do."

"What do you mean?"

"Men can't always grasp this concept," Laura said, "but if a man is willing to use violence, he's willing to use violence. I'm sure you know what I mean."

I told her I did know what she meant.

"If I had to guess—and this would only be a guess—I'd say that Johanna was waiting for the right moment to leave him. And maybe . . ."

I remained quiet. Laura shook her head.

"Now I'm just using my imagination," she said.

"Go ahead. Anything at all might help."

She shook her head again.

"This is going to sound crazy," she said, not sounding the least bit crazy, "but maybe when she looked at him, or stood next to him, she felt self-conscious somehow, felt like she almost understood something about him—Tarkiainen, I mean—that she couldn't say at the time, even though she ought to say it, needed to say it. But that's pure speculation, of course. I can't really remember anything like that."

"Thank you."

"I don't know if that helps."

"It helps a lot," I said, as warmly and friendly as I knew how to be, which was easy, because I had a sincere desire to thank her. "It helps in a lot of ways. I'm glad I came to see you."

I got up from my chair, as did she. I felt a fleeting confusion—like I was living in two different times, twenty years ago and today. Luckily the feeling quickly passed. I stepped toward her, took her hand, which felt surprisingly familiar in mine, and held it a moment. When I let go, I wrapped my arms around her.

Twenty years, and my arms didn't reach any farther than they ever had.

17

HAMID'S TAXI WAS AROUND THE CORNER WITH THE MOTOR RUNning, just a hundred meters away. I sped up my steps so that I wouldn't get wet, but I got wet anyway. The rain was falling in sheets that the wind tossed where it would. A gust of rain hit me in the face with easily enough water to wash my hair. I got to the taxi, opened the door, and climbed in. Hamid turned nearly 180 degrees in the driver's seat and laughed out loud when he saw how wet I was.

"It's raining pretty hard," he said cheerfully.

"It's raining pretty hard," I agreed. I asked him to drive me home. On the way I explained that I would need his services for some time and that I would, of course, pay for them. This suited Hamid, and after a little dickering we agreed on a price. I leaned back in my seat, gave my wet hair a finger fluff, and, after some hesitation, tried Johanna's number. Not available.

Next I called Jaatinen. He didn't answer so I left a message asking him to get in touch with me as soon as possible.

I reached Elina and asked her to have Ahti call me as soon as he was up and about.

Hamid wove his way down the Sörnäinen shore road looking for a faster lane, but not finding one. Every time he sped up to move into a promising-looking opening the traffic slowed to a nearly pedestrian pace again. Hamid was a young man and drove like young men always have, with no concern for saving gas or saving lives. Both were getting cheaper by the day.

The oil hadn't run out yet, although they'd been predicting it would for decades. The problem was, in fact, the opposite. There was enough oil to do everything that had accelerated the rise of the sea levels; enough to destroy the air, land, and water for good; enough to pollute all the lakes, rivers, and seas; enough to continue to manufacture all the same useless junk. Those who had been afraid we would run out of oil had the satisfaction of knowing that the supply just kept on coming. It wouldn't die. When the world ended one day we would still have tankers full of oil, ports full of it, billions of barrels of black gold, ample fuel for a trip to eternity.

Hamid found a lane that was moving. We drove onto Kulosaari bridge, and the traffic was nearly stopped again at the other end. The right lane, on the sea side, was closed, and we inched forward at a snail's pace. The flashing light of a fire truck dyed the rain blue like a scene from a horror story, and far up ahead we could see a truck with its cab still on the bridge and its trailer crashed through the side of an office building. From a distance it looked at first like nothing remarkable, as if the truck were somehow simply driving out of the building and onto the bridge.

From up close, the situation was different, of course. The ambulances that had been hidden a moment earlier by the fire trucks were waiting with their doors open so that at least some of the pedestrians and office workers hit by the truck could be placed onto stretchers and receive some kind of treatment. We passed the scene of the accident in silence, neither of us speaking. Soon we had sped up again and passed through Kulosaari and into Herttoniemi.

When we got to my building I dug the payment we'd agreed on out of my pocket, and Hamid backed out of the driveway and pulled away. He had promised to be there within fifteen minutes if and when I called.

The quiet, empty apartment seemed even sadder now, as if it, too, were tense and worried, and no longer knew how to be cozy, warm, and safe. I took off my shoes and put my wet coat on a hook before I had to sit down on the swivel stool next to the door. I just barely managed to grab hold of the seat of the stool before the tears came. Tears, the first I'd shed in years, flooding from my eyes, hot and heavy on my cheeks.

I was worn out. It felt like everything was pointless, like every effort to take hold of something was just futile groping. I had disappointed myself and betrayed Johanna's trust. I replayed all the promises I'd made to her—I'll always help you, I'll always love you, I'll do anything to make things easier for you.

Calm down, Tapani, I told myself. You can keep your promises, even if you can't deliver right now.

I let the tears come—let the worry and grief swell and then subside again. I don't really know how long I sat there. It seemed like a long time.

When I could finally move again, I tried not to look around me. Everything in the apartment reminded me of Johanna and made me wonder why I couldn't figure out where she could be.

I took off my clothes and got in the shower. I noticed that

I was doing everything hurriedly, in swift swipes—shampoo, shower gel, shaving. I tried to count to ten as I shaved. I got to three.

I wasn't all that ready for what I might find in the clothes closet. As I was taking a clean pair of socks out of the wardrobe, my eye fell on a bit of red and gold wrapping paper. My Christmas gift for Johanna. I took the package out of the closet, laid it on the bed, and looked at it. I stood there with a sock on one foot, unable to decide what to do next. It's strange how the meanings of things can change. It wasn't a handwritten, hand-bound book of poems and a modest amount of mad money lying there on the bed, it was our whole life. Everything that makes a life out of each day. I felt the tears rising to my eyes again, then hot, large tears rolling down my face to my lips and chin.

I turned, put a sock on my other foot, and walked out of the bedroom, leaving the gift where it lay.

I made some coffee, took Johanna's cup from the counter and put it in the cupboard, got out my own, and sat down with it at the computer. I went through everything again but didn't find anything new or useful. I looked at the surveillance footage from the corner of Fredrikinkatu and Urho Kekkosen katu and still didn't see anything that caught my attention.

I poured myself some more coffee, had an idea, and used Johanna's password to search through archives for articles she'd written for various papers and magazines. I looked through them all as thoroughly as I had the Healer memos until I was out of coffee and had to get up and walk around. My ribs didn't ache constantly anymore. The clubbing I'd got made itself known only when I sat in certain positions.

I tried to call Chief Inspector Jaatinen again, but he still wasn't answering. I went back to the computer to read some more of Johanna's articles.

Johanna wrote for many different publications and had always been a diligent writer, particularly when she was a young freelancer. She wrote quickly and clearly and built up people's trust, including the people she interviewed—all the characteristics of a good journalist. But her real talent lay in finding little connections, or big ones, amid all the details, and summing them up. I wished I had that quality.

Amid all the uncertainty and searching, I had progressed in my investigation, such as it was. What Laura had told me, for instance, had confirmed my idea of Johanna and Pasi Tarkiainen's youthful relationship. And what I'd learned from Elina about Johanna's complete silence on the subject told me that she had been afraid, and she'd had good reason to be afraid, from what I could tell.

So why was I so jealous?

And why did it feel so terrible?

I was jealous because I felt that something had been kept secret from me. But the jealousy felt unpleasant and crushingly petty. Families were being murdered, and I was fretting about whether my feelings should be hurt. It was humbling to realize I could be more childish and self-centered than I had ever imagined.

And the wretched feeling wasn't helped by the fact that now, with jealousy burning inside me and paranoia flowing freely, my eyes were drawn to the glowing, inviting e-mail icon on Johanna's computer screen.

18

Jaatinen's face was wet from the rain, red from the sea wind, and, it seemed to me, purposely inscrutable. We were standing on the sea side of Jätkäsaari, a couple of hundred meters north of the place where my ribs and back had got a taste of the security guards' clubs and boots. The wind pushed its cold claws under my parka and through the fabric of my pants, then gusted away. I would have been shivering with cold if I wasn't already shaking from shock.

Moments earlier, Jaatinen had taken me to the six-story waterfront building behind us, to an open, clean, quietly tasteful penthouse apartment where a banker and his family lay murdered.

Jaatinen looked at the sea, searching for something in the gray-green surface of the water and looking more like he was postponing what he had to say than pondering it.

What can a person say in a situation like that? A lot, no doubt, but words escaped me. I had never seen anything like it. And nothing can prepare you for it. Nothing, I said to myself.

"The reason I asked you to come here, of course, is our

suspicion of Tarkiainen. To find out the new information you have on him."

I told him about my visit to Tarkiainen's former hangout, about my theories concerning him, and my conversations with people who knew him.

"It's all unofficial, of course," Jaatinen said.

"Of course," I said, and swallowed.

No matter how hard I tried to put the murder scene out of my mind, I couldn't. The bloodied hair, the bedding, the dark stains on the wall, the small bodies under the blankets. What had they been thinking about when they went to bed? The games they played that day? Opening presents?

"How did they—" I began, not knowing how to put it. "How did they keep sleeping with someone walking around shooting at them?"

"That's exactly the reason that Tarkiainen is the name we're most interested in. He knows something about medicine. He probably knows what to use to make a person sleep, and how to administer it. But we won't know for sure until the lab tests and technical investigation is complete. And as I said, we're somewhat at a loss with our staff shortage, although this case is serious enough that it'll be a high priority, I think. Things being as they are, we won't get an answer for a few days, in any case, perhaps a few weeks."

His voice faded off. I didn't know how to continue, so I just waited for him to take up the thread again. There was a boat dock ahead on the right behind a high fence topped with barbed wire. The long, narrow dock was empty now. It stretched out its light-brown arm toward the sea as if beckoning to someone. On the other side of the barbed wire was a guard's booth the size of a summer cabin that would be manned again when spring came, assuming that there were enough people in the area of sufficient means to afford a boat.

"This is purely hypothetical, of course," Jaatinen said when we'd been quiet for altogether too long, considering the bile rising in my throat, the stinging wind that had us at its mercy, and the general panic I was feeling.

"And absolutely unofficial," I managed to say.

"That goes without saying," Jaatinen said. "In theory the order of events might have been as follows: Suppose someone in the family needs a doctor. They go online and request a doctor visit. Someone on the lookout for that very thing diverts or intercepts their message. Pasi Tarkiainen shows up and says he's the doctor. He uses a false name, since anyone can check online databases and see that there is no one named Pasi Tarkiainen who's a doctor, that, in fact, Pasi Tarkiainen has been dead for years. But keep in mind that that's exactly what people don't do—they don't check things out, even when their own health or safety is at stake. That's one way that things haven't changed."

He took a breath and seemed to gather his thoughts, squeezing the bridge of his nose between his thumb and forefinger. I saw the bloody sheets again, the puddle of congealed blood under the child's bed, the bloody tuft of hair on the white surface of the night table.

"Tarkiainen pretends to be a doctor, examines the patient as he ought to, prescribes medication, and then tells them that now would be a good time to inoculate them all against malaria or something. Who would say no, if a doctor suggested it? He inoculates them, but not with what he said exactly. He gives them some kind of long-lasting sedative that doesn't take effect right away. A few hours later, the one who does the dirty work has a clear path. He gets the door code from Tarkiainen, maybe even a key card, gets into the apartment, where they're all asleep, and—"

"Shoots them, one by one," I said.

"Yes."

We stood another moment in the thrashing wind. The cement-gray sky rose from the horizon over our heads up into invisibility. A black and brown mongrel dog ran along the beach alone. A few gray and white gulls moved lazily, dutifully out of its way.

"That's quite a hypothesis," I said.

"Just a hypothesis," Jaatinen answered.

"But knowing what we know now . . ."

"Exactly. Maybe it's not just a hypothesis," he said, nodding. "There's a warrant out for Tarkiainen's arrest. It doesn't mean anything, practically speaking, but he doesn't know that. Maybe it'll ring some bells somewhere. It's not terribly likely it will, but at the moment it feels like Tarkiainen's not nearly as dead as he was a little while ago."

Jaatinen took out a cotton handkerchief and wiped his eyes. We were quiet again. We were getting used to that. He stuffed the handkerchief back in the pocket of his beige overcoat and straightened up to his full height.

"I have to ask," I said. "Why did you show that to me? Why did I need to see the heads blown to pieces and the puddles of blood under the bed?"

He looked at me.

"You wanted to be a part of this," he said, and turned to face the sea.

I watched him and thought at first that he was looking at some specific point, trying to get a glimpse of something. But his gaze only seemed to be aimed at the horizon. It actually was falling like a stone into the water, somewhere far out at sea.

"And you're on Tarkiainen's trail. It's better if you know what it is we're talking about. You're quite close."

He dropped his gaze again until it barely reached the water's edge.

"But think about this. Whenever some lunatic gets it in his head that a few individuals are responsible for the world falling apart around him, we go after him. And what happens when we catch him? Some new lunatic comes along, and the world keeps marching toward destruction. That's nothing new, of course. History tells us that this kind of thing has happened many times before. Civilization blossoms and then it falls. It's happened on this planet in our own lifetime, to millions and millions of people, even before now. But you take it harder, somehow, when it's your own little world that's dying. Don't you, Tapani?"

"I guess so."

A large black-hulled boat appeared on the open sea, on its way to somewhere. I watched it for a moment, then I saw the blood again, the blankets, the little head of brown hair, broken in two. Evil and senseless. I couldn't see anything else. I had to get away.

19

In spite of the shock and feeling so sick, I fell asleep in the backseat of the taxi. Dreams came in swift waves, like seizures. In the clearest of the dreams, Johanna was whispering something into Laura Vuola's ear, both of them looking at me, afraid and angry. Johanna held her hand in front of her face so that I couldn't see her lips moving, but I could tell from the expression on Laura's face and the direction of her gaze that they were talking about me. I felt a swift, altogether irrational sting of jealousy, then I woke up. I couldn't get the dream out of my mind at first, and sat groggily wondering what they had been saying.

I finally came fully awake when Hamid slammed on the brakes and I was thrown against my seat belt. The strap locked up, and I felt a pain in my side. When the car had come to a complete stop I was able to get my breath and loosen the seat belt. We were behind a bus, with mere millimeters between our bumpers.

"Sorry," Hamid said. "That was a rough stop."

"It's OK," I said, looking around.

We were on our way to Munkkiniemi. At the moment, though, we were stopped at a busy intersection waiting for our turn to move into the passing lane.

The rain had let up, replaced by a fog that filled the space between the earth and sky and was so thick in places that the cars nearby disappeared, leaving nothing to show their existence but their white headlights and red and yellow taillights. When we started moving again, the whole world seemed to be made up of vague, fragmented bits like a poor-quality video broadcast—the car that was over there is now here, there was a house there but now it's gone, a light is flashing beside us, and now it's moved in front of us.

I looked at my phone and quickly went through the files I'd saved about Tarkiainen. I'd looked at them cursorily before. I hadn't noticed that there weren't four addresses for Tarkiainen, but five. I hadn't noticed it because two of his former addresses were the same—he had lived in the same apartment in Munkkiniemi at two different times, first about twenty years ago, for two years, and then again in the year before his death.

Hamid found the house quickly, parked on the street, and listened with a friendly, patient look as I explained again that I would need him to stay here and not take another fare.

"I understand, I understand," he said with a sigh, and I stopped explaining.

It made him smile.

I left his smile in the rearview mirror, got out of the car, and walked across the asphalt driveway to the door of the building. A soft, almost imperceptible breeze stirred the columns of mist like slow-motion cotton candy. As I walked I could see the fog open in front of me and close behind me.

It was a 1930s-era building, in good condition from the look of it—the beautiful wood grain running over the surface of the door was freshly lacquered. There was a brightly lit name directory on the wall to the left of the door, each name followed by a buzzer. None of them meant anything to me. I pushed a few buzzers at random: Saarinen, Bonsdorff, Niemelä, Kataja.

Bonsdorff answered.

I pulled the door open and looked behind me. The fog was so thick that if I hadn't known Hamid's taxi was parked on the street, I would have had to go look for it. According to the directory, Bonsdorff was on the fourth floor. I pushed the button for the elevator, rode it up, and twisted the old-fashioned metal bell on a door with a mail slot that read BONSDORFF.

The point of light in the door's peephole darkened momentarily, then the door opened. Bonsdorff, it seemed, was Mrs. Bonsdorff, a woman at least eighty years old.

"I've been waiting for you," she said.

I didn't know what else to say but "I'm sorry you had to wait."

"These days?" she said with a snort. "Come on in."

She turned and walked into the apartment. I didn't know who she'd been waiting for, but since she'd opened the door and told me to come in, I obeyed.

It was a large apartment, five rooms and a kitchen, from what I could tell at a glance. Mrs. Bonsdorff looked and sounded like she lived there alone. A glimpse into a couple of rooms confirmed the impression: they seemed to be unused, the requisite quilt at the foot of the bed and decorative pillows had been put where they were a long time ago. I followed her into the living-dining room and waited for her to stop and tell me who she'd been waiting for and perhaps let me tell her why I was there.

She walked across a black and burgundy Oriental rug the

size of a squash court. It was so big I was sure someone must have got lost on it at some point. She went to the television and knocked her small fist against it a couple of times.

"Here it is," she said. "No picture."

I looked at the television and then at Mrs. Bonsdorff. She was a short woman with curly hair, dressed elegantly in a gray blazer even at home, radiating resolve and energy in spite of her age and stooped posture.

I thought for a moment.

What harm could it do?

I walked across the squash court to the television, checked to make sure the cords were attached, and tried to turn it on.

"It doesn't work," she informed me.

I looked at the cords again and noticed that one of them was hanging slack. I followed it under an antique bureau of dark wood and behind a rococo sofa, and found that it had come unplugged. I plugged it in and went back over to the television. The picture appeared immediately.

"I could have done that myself," she said.

I switched it off again and turned to look at her.

"Shall we agree that I won't take any payment if you answer a couple of questions?"

Something flashed in her eyes.

"I should have known," she said. "What repairman comes on the same day you request him nowadays? Would you like some coffee?"

We drank coffee from porcelain cups at the dining room table. Mrs. Bonsdorff wore a gold and diamond ring on her left hand, touching it and turning it on her finger regularly, habitually, laying the diamond against her little finger and then straightening it again as she spoke. This made me aware of my own wedding ring, a thick band of white gold with a level edge. I'd put it on my finger ten years ago, threaded through with the woman I was searching for, a search that had brought me here.

The coffee was dark, strong, chocolatey. I realized I'd been craving a cup of coffee. I also realized that I couldn't have drunk a thing one second earlier. I pushed the images from the apartment in Jätkäsaari out of my mind again.

I told her I was looking for a man who had once lived in her building, described Tarkiainen to her, told her his name and profession, and added that it was possible I was in the wrong building. Finally, I showed her the picture of him on my phone. She went stiff and assured me that I was in the right building.

"I remember him very well," she said.

"He died five years ago," I said.

She looked confused.

"Five years ago?"

I nodded.

She held on to the small porcelain handle of her cup as if she might pinch it off.

"At my age the years go by a bit faster, of course, but it couldn't have been five years ago."

"Why?" I asked.

"Because it was just before Erik died," she said. "My husband. He died of liver cancer. It started as throat and stomach cancer. He was in terrible pain, pain beyond description."

Her searching gaze drifted out the window into the fog.

"I loved Erik. We had nothing left but each other," she said quietly, and took a sip of coffee. I took a cookie from the saucer on the table, bit off a small piece, and let the toffee flavor dissolve in my mouth. She set her cup in its saucer with a clink.

"Erik was an athletic man, a good man, a strong man. At least as long as he was able. But no one can be strong when age and sickness come, when there's not much time left. Our children and grandchildren all live in America. We keep in touch with video calls. It just makes me miss them more. I'm old enough to feel that I ought to be able to touch them, be near them, pet them and hug them and hold them, and have them hold me. Erik was the same way. We were there for each other, took care of each other."

She paused for a moment, sank deeper into the fog, then realized she had, and turned to look at me again.

"Are you married?" she asked.

"Yes," I said, and quickly added, "actually, that's why I'm here today."

She looked curious.

"My wife is missing," I said. "This man, the man I was asking you about, might know something about it. It's not really him that I'm looking for, but my wife."

"Do you have any children?"

"No."

"May I ask why?"

"Yes. We couldn't have children."

She seemed to ponder my answer.

"Just the two of you."

"Yes."

"That's good, too."

I felt something rough in my throat and wiped my eyes just in case.

"Yes, it is," I said.

We sat across the table from each other, two people randomly thrown together, and I had an almost tangible feeling of how much the two of us had in common. How much all of us have in common. I didn't want to break the silence that also united us. It felt strangely calming, almost final. I didn't want to pry, to interrogate her. Maybe she would eventually circle back to what I had come to ask her about.

I tasted the strong coffee and let it gently sting my tongue before I swallowed it. I looked at the pictures on the wall—seascapes sparkling with sunshine, country houses painted red and yellow, glowing golden fields and dark green forests. Fantasy places.

"Erik's pain seemed to increase as quickly as his medication," she said. I had just been wandering in the wind-rippled wheat, about to open the gray-timbered house dimly visible at one side of a field. "The cancer was progressing, of course. And that's when the young man offered to help us."

"How did he offer to help?"

She thought for a moment.

"Now that you ask, it was really quite surprising. How did he know to come here when the situation was at its worst? He was just at the door one day."

"When did this happen?" I asked, putting my empty cup down in its saucer.

"Erik died a year ago," she said. "He came about six months before that. That's why I don't understand—you said that the young man died five years ago, but a man of the same name, who looked the same, who I thought was a doctor, came here a year and a half ago and said he wanted to help us."

She was clearly flustered.

"There's nothing wrong with your memory," I said. "It's my mistake. I must have had incorrect information, that's all."

"That must be it," she said, looking for a moment even older than she was. "It frightens me. If I lose my memory—lose my mind—what will I have left?"

"You have nothing to worry about," I assured her. "Your memory is excellent. Tell me more about this man, the one who showed up a year and a half ago. Did he ever mention why he had come?"

"That's another thing," she said. "It wasn't for money. He never took any payment for his time and didn't even want much money for the medicine. Erik was so sick by then that we needed all the medication we could get for him. Things we hadn't been able to get."

"And this man helped you?"

"Yes. I was grateful to him. He also helped Erik on his final journey."

"Here at home?"

"What better place to die?"

I saw the place at Jätkäsaari again. Human forms under a blanket. Bloodstains on the wall above the bed.

"No better place, I guess," I said. "Then what happened?"

She looked at me.

"Then Erik was cremated and I was left alone after forty-six years," she said.

"I'm sorry. And after that?"

She looked impatient now.

"I would have liked to die, but I didn't die," she said. "Sometimes it's that simple."

"Forgive me, Mrs. Bonsdorff," I said quietly. "I didn't mean that. Perhaps I didn't say it very well. I mean, what about this doctor, Tarkiainen? Did you ever hear from him again?"

"He disappeared the same way he had come. He arrived uninvited and left without saying good-bye. I've never heard from him again."

"Do you know whether he lived in this building at the time he was helping Erik?"

She pondered the question.

"I hadn't thought about it. I suppose it's possible. It's certainly not impossible."

"Did you ever run into him on the stairs or in the courtyard?"

She shook her head, slowly but with certainty.

"I don't think so. Of course . . ."

"Yes?"

"Now that I think about it, I may have wondered at the time how he could get here so quickly after we called him, and in his shirtsleeves, with just his bag in his hand. But I didn't think any more about it at the time."

I didn't know in which direction my questions should go. I wiped my lips with the small napkin she'd given me, although they were already painfully dry.

"Are you and your wife happy?" she asked abruptly.

I looked deep into her blue-green eyes, so much like Johanna's that for a fraction of a second I almost fell into them.

"I've never loved anyone or anything as much as I love my wife," I heard myself say. Mrs. Bonsdorff's gaze never faltered. Deep creases appeared in her cheeks, at the edges of her eyes. A warm smile rose to her face, and I could see that they were her eyes and not Johanna's.

I WAS IN THE foyer putting on my coat and looking at myself in the large, gilt-framed mirror when she said, "When you find your wife . . ."

I turned and looked at her. She was nearly swallowed by the large entrance to the living room and the dense fog outside the window.

"Don't lose her again."

I tied my scarf around my neck.

"I'll do my best, Mrs. Bonsdorff."

I had already turned away from her and put my right hand on the door handle and my left on the lock when I heard her say: "It's not easy, but it's worth it."

20

I LOOKED AT THE DIRECTORY AGAIN FOR THE BUILDING MANAGER'S apartment number. It was on the first floor, someone named Jakolev. There was no answer. Maybe they weren't home, or maybe they were just keeping quiet on the other side of the door. I could hear myself breathing, and water in the pipes somewhere, and smell the heavy, rotten smell of fried eggs. I waited a moment, then found the phone number on the directory and tried calling. Jakolev didn't answer. I was getting used to no one answering my calls, I guess. I slipped the phone back into my pocket and left.

When I got outside I filled my lungs with air, opened the door of the taxi, and got in, waking Hamid.

"Where to now?" he asked, looking more alert in a second than I ever did.

I thought about where to go, what place made sense. And about what I knew for certain now: Tarkiainen was alive.

Johanna had been on the trail of the Healer.

Tarkiainen had some connection with the Healer.

Tarkiainen and Johanna had met.

That's as far as I'd got when Hamid turned and looked at me with his dark, nearly black eyes.

"Where do you want to go?" he asked.

At that moment my phone beeped, telling me I had a message. I took it out, read the message, and immediately knew where to go.

On the way, Hamid stopped at a service station. He hopped lightly out of the car, went to the pump, inserted his card and keyed in his code, and started to fill up. I got out of the car, too, got a blast of heady, metallic gasoline fumes, and walked the couple of steps to the counter. The fog was still thick, and the air felt stagnant and damp on my skin.

The former culinary school behind the service station stood silent, its windows black. There were about a dozen people milling around in front of it, men and women who communicated through roars, grunts, and half-syllable shouts. They had a plastic bottle that they were passing around and lifting to their lips.

A large, high SUV with darkened windows pulled into the station on the other side of the pump. Both the driver's and the passenger's doors opened and two Slavic-looking men the size of bulldozers appeared and dropped to the ground. One of them went to the gas pump and the other stood next to the car. I couldn't see inside the car, but I made an educated guess that there was a man in the backseat who would never be able to spend all his money.

The service station was the world in miniature: petroleum under the ground, the masses in their vehicles, and a few who enriched themselves on the distress of the rest. I suppose we all had our place here at this gas station, and in the universe.

Hamid put the nozzle back on the side of the pump with

a clank, waking me from my thoughts. His timing was excellent because the bulldozer guarding the car had noticed me staring and, judging by his expression, was about to come over and ask me if I had anything to say to him. And I couldn't honestly say that I did.

Hamid backed the taxi up from the pump and headed toward the center of town.

The plaza at the train station was nearly full of people and cars. Hamid dropped me off in front of the shopping center across from the station. I dodged people, went into the café, and got in line. While I waited I heard bits of conversation in at least ten different languages. Some of them I understood, most I didn't. I bought a coffee and a sandwich that was so tightly wrapped in thin paper that only the golden-brown tip told me that it was some kind of bread. I paid and looked around for someplace to sit. I got lucky when an African family gathered its coats and bags and headed toward the railway station.

I sat down, and when a man with a broad smile asked in Spanish-accented English if he could have the extra chairs, I told him yes, except for one. One was saved for Johanna's editor, Lassi Uutela. I didn't say that part out loud.

The roll was dry and contained the thinnest slice of cheese I'd ever seen. Had it been any thinner, I wouldn't have seen it.

I'd finished the sandwich and coffee when Lassi arrived.

He shook my hand, glanced into my eyes only in passing, pulled out a chair, threw his left leg over his right, slapped his hair into place, and ran a hand over the stubble on his face. Then he picked up his spoon and stirred his coffee.

He looked as tired and world-weary as he had the day before, but I understood better now that his battered, worn-out appearance was a kind of armor that made it easier to make decisions, to play for time, and to conceal his own thoughts and their resulting actions. The whole image of the exhausted but tough newspaperman, red around the eyes, his beard always at the right stage of stubble, was just a role made to measure for an experienced player.

"I've got a pretty tight day today," he said. He nodded toward his offices across the street. "The place is in chaos. A lot of articles just about to come together. That's why I suggested meeting here. Get a little peace."

"Right," I said, and looked around me. The people of all ages and colors, the multitude of languages, and the clatter of the café made it a pleasant place to meet, of course, but it certainly would have been more peaceful someplace else. "I haven't looked at this morning's paper, but I'm sure there must have been an article about that singer and her horse you were talking about yesterday."

Lassi still didn't look me in the eye.

"Did you want to praise me for a successful piece of journalism?"

He slurped his coffee, the cup steady in his hand, his eyes not evading mine by a millimeter now.

"Why not meet at your office?" I asked.

"Like I said," he sighed, putting his cup gently on the table and pushing it a few centimeters away from him, "it's more peaceful here."

"First you don't answer my calls, then when I send a message that I'm coming to your office, you call and suggest we meet somewhere else. It makes me wonder—who's at your office who isn't supposed to see me?"

He looked at me questioningly, again with that tired skepticism that said he was perhaps a bit intrigued, but also convinced that I was an imbecile and a nuisance.

"Who isn't supposed to know that Johanna's missing, and her husband's looking for her?" I asked.

He didn't speak for a moment.

"Keep on babbling," he said. "I don't know what you're talking about."

"OK, let's forget that for a moment. Tell me why you called me to tell me Gromov was dead."

Lassi looked at me almost pityingly.

"I was trying to help," he said.

"That's all?"

"That's all," he repeated with a sigh.

"I don't remember exactly how you put it, but you said something about how much you value your employees."

"It's true," he said.

"Then tell me why Johanna's disappearance hasn't caused you to act. You know that Gromov is dead. You have reason to believe that Johanna is in at least some kind of trouble. You have reason to believe that the trouble she's in might have something to do with the family murders she was writing about."

"You're a poet, Tapani. A journalist would get to the heart of the matter, think about what the truth is, and report on it. You're building stories, fairy tales. You're making things up. On the other hand, imagination is a good thing. We need it these days."

"No editor would pass up a story like this," I said.

"I don't see any story in it."

"You don't want to see one. And I want to know why."

Lassi leaned back in his chair.

"You sound like your wife," he said. "And that's not a compliment."

"What have you got against Johanna?"

He shook his head.

"The question is, what has Johanna got against me?"

"Your attitude, for one thing, I would imagine."

"I'm trying to put out a newspaper."

"And Johanna's not?"

"Not the same newspaper. I told you what our situation is. Some people get it, and some people don't."

"And Johanna didn't?"

I glanced outside. The fog looked like it was pressing against the windows, trying to get in.

"Not at all," Lassi said, leaning still farther back. "We're living in rather difficult times, in many ways, but one thing is beginning to become clear. The kind of truth that a few journalists like Johanna are still looking for just doesn't exist anymore. There's nothing to rest it on, nothing to base it on, nothing to cultivate it. I could talk for a long time about the end of history, the disappearance of values, the pornographication of everything. But stuffed shirts like you know better. It was what it was. We're trying to put out a paper in the environment we're in now. I have a blank page that I have to fill with pictures and text that looks like news, something that will interest people. And what are people interested in? Today it's an R&B singer and her horse. Tomorrow it's a celebrity caught shoplifting and exposing herself, if it's up to me. We have surveillance photos, close-ups almost, of this woman stuffing an MP3 player in her underwear, and while she's at it you can see practically everything, if you know what I mean."

"Congratulations," I said.

"You think you can afford to be sarcastic? You're a poet whose most successful collection sold less than two hundred copies. We sell at least two hundred thousand papers a day."

"You're relieved that Johanna's missing."

"Relieved is the wrong word," Lassi said, shaking his head.

"There's more to it than that," I said.

"Of course there is," he said with a laugh. There was more than a touch of superiority in his laugh. He looked at me in amusement. "You can imagine what you want. Write a book of poems and put all your crazy imaginings in there."

I leaned forward and put my elbows on the table.

"I know that Pasi Tarkiainen is a friend of yours. Or a former friend, at least."

He stopped. There was a crack in his practiced, weary expression, a brief glimpse of uncertainty, before his jaded outer shell remembered to cover it up. I mentally thanked Jaatinen for giving me the information.

Lassi looked at me for a moment before he spoke.

"Former friend."

"You played on the same floor hockey team," I said.

"On the one hand I'm amazed that a scribbler like you found something like that out, but on the other hand I'm rather frustrated. You know why?"

I shook my head, spread my arms.

"No matter how I try," he said, "I can't see any sense in all this. So what if I played floor hockey with the guy—what was his name again?"

"You don't remember his name? A moment ago you were sure that he was an old friend of yours."

Lassi sighed, once again safe within his role—the weary, worn-out newspaperman. He folded his arms across his chest.

"Pasi Tarkiainen was a friend of yours and you also worked together in radical activities," I said. "I found out about the floor hockey by accident, by doing an Internet search for your name and Tarkiainen's together. I found out from other sources that you were part of one of the most extreme environmental groups. Tarkiainen joined when you two already knew each other, didn't he? You were young—young enough to think that bombs could change things. Metaphorically and literally."

Lassi looked at me, his face locked in that one familiar expression that masked whatever he might be thinking or feeling. I continued: "And when a bomb went off at the offices of Fortum Energy fifteen years ago, you were one of the people questioned. So was Tarkiainen. Neither of you was ever indicted, however, and nothing was found to connect you to the crime. Nevertheless, it's not the kind of thing an editor wants people to know about him. You can hardly put such a thing on your résumé: Fortum Energy bombing, such and such a year."

He looked out the window before speaking.

"Someone once said that a person who isn't idealistic in his youth hasn't lived and a person who isn't conservative in his old age hasn't learned anything from his life. I might add that by 'conservative' I mean realistic, recognizing reality. And your information is correct in the sense that I was a young idealist. As far as the rest of it, I would respectfully suggest that you go fuck yourself."

I nodded and asked softly, "So did Tarkiainen the young idealist turn out to be a cynical shit like you?"

Lassi had regained his superior smile, and he used it.

"Pasi Tarkiainen died years ago. Whether he died an idealist or a cynical shit I don't know and I don't care. And, anyway, what does he have to do with anything?"

"Maybe a lot. And you're lying again. How long have you known that Tarkiainen isn't dead?"

Lassi's grin contracted a little at the edges. He scratched the bridge of his nose. He looked like he might be a little nervous.

"Is that a trick question?"

"No," I said. "It's a straightforward question, and it has to do with Johanna. It has to do with your reluctance to invest in finding her and your sudden lack of interest in publishing a story that would almost certainly bring in readers. Just think of it—families brutally murdered, an ambitious reporter vanished, police stupefied. A textbook case of media appeal. Is Tarkiainen blackmailing you?"

Lassi laughed, but it was a feeble laugh this time. He didn't answer, and he didn't look me in the eye.

"Last question," I said. "Let's go back to the beginning: Why couldn't we meet at your office?"

21

Johanna was working the first time we met. She was writing an article about the closing of the libraries, and I happened to be one of the people she interviewed.

"Do you come here often?" she asked as we stood in the foyer of the Kallio library during its last week in operation. I was struck by how she had worded her question.

I seized the opportunity and said, "Haven't we met somewhere before?"

She blushed the way that she always did—just a fleeting trace of pink. She wrote my answers in her notebook, thanked me, and was turning to leave when I asked her how often she came to the library.

She smiled a little and turned to face me again.

"A couple of times a week," she said.

That's when I really noticed her eyes. They seemed to gather all the sunlight that filtered through the tall, many-paned windows into the library. It felt like all the light in the dimming, fast-darkening world was shining from this young journalist's eyes.

"What do you like to read?" I asked.

She thought for a moment.

"Mostly nonfiction, I guess," she said, looking like she was really thinking about it. "Things connected with my work. Directly or indirectly."

"What about history?"

"Sometimes."

"Novels?"

"Sometimes."

"Poetry?"

"Never."

"Why not?"

"It's annoying. Particularly newer poetry. Deliberately, willfully obscure. 'Heart's blood on a hammer's handle striking eternal moonlight as the gentle hoof handkerchief lashes its licorice temples.' Who can read something like that and pretend they get something out of it?"

"OK," I said. "Can you remember the names of any poets or books of poems you've read?"

She looked at me with those wondrous eyes, named a couple of books of poems, and shook her head. I said I agreed with her that the poems she mentioned were obscure, but I thought that there were some good poems, too, that I knew of a few excellent collections that I was sure would change her opinion or at least make her realize that an entire genre of literature she was rejecting did include some exceptions.

"Do you read that stuff?" she asked in slight disbelief.

"Yes, I read that stuff," I said, with the emphasis on the last two words.

We smiled at each other for a moment, the light dancing in her eyes.

"I'll bet you could recommend a book to me, to make me change my mind."

"Maybe," I said.

She followed me to the poetry section of the library. I could feel her eyes on the back of my neck. The feeling was not unpleasant. I thought about the blue-green light shining from this woman's eyes and settling on me like the light of a rainbow or a bright, sunny day.

We came to the poetry shelves and I picked out a few Finnish poets' works, putting one of my own books on the bottom of the pile. Johanna came and stood next to me and listened, if not with interest, at least with the appearance of interest, as I told her about each poet's characteristic qualities and read her one poem from each to demonstrate the clarity and conciseness of their language.

She was wearing wide-legged jeans, a black turtleneck sweater, and some kind of combination of a leather shoe and a boot. And as we stood close to each other, I couldn't help but smell the scent of her hair, sense the warmth from her body, and feel the pull of those light-collecting, blue-green eyes.

I grabbed the last book in the stack, opened it, and read a poem. When I had finished, I looked at her. She didn't look as impressed as I had hoped she would be.

"I don't know," she said.

"Shall I read another one?"

"Go ahead."

I read another.

"You seem to know it by heart," she said. "You said it without looking at the book."

She took the book out of my hands, opened it, and saw my photo on the inside cover. She raised her eyes.

"Very clever," she said with a smile.

22

I STOOD FOR A MOMENT ON THE SIDEWALK AND WATCHED HAMID'S taillights disappear into the fog.

On the short drive from the train station to Temppeliaukio, I had time to think about the tenacious strands that held us all together: Johanna, Pasi Tarkiainen, Lassi Uutela, Laura Vuola, Harri Jaatinen, and me. Even Mrs. Bonsdorff and Hamid. Not to mention Ahti and Elina. We run, straining, gasping, and groaning, in our own separate directions, and the more we struggle the closer we're pulled together.

Elina opened the door. She greeted me with a warm smile and had an almost questioning look on her face for a moment. I got a glimpse of myself in the entryway mirror and realized why. My eyes were shining in a way that could be interpreted as anger, even rage. I didn't want to explain it to her—I didn't really think I could. At least not yet. I said that I wanted to see Ahti.

"Ahti's asleep."

"Wake him up."

"I'm sorry?"

"Wake him up."

She looked at me in amazement, then with apparent annoyance. Finally she granted my wish and walked toward the bedroom shaking her head.

Everything in the living room was as familiar as it could be. I knew Ahti and Elina's bookshelf by heart. The books and their arrangement had been etched into my mind over the dozens of times that we had all sat in this room together. I knew without touching it how soft and enveloping the black armchair was that sat in front of it, how bright the floor lamp was that stood next to it. I remembered an evening we'd spent together that stretched into the night, the candles and candle holders rummaged out of the dark brown antique chest huddled on the other side of the chair with a book lying open on its lid, as always.

Although the room was familiar, I looked at all of it as if for the first time as I listened to the noises coming from the bedroom. I thought about how it's not the things that are new to us that surprise us, it's the things we think we know and find out we don't.

"He'll be here in a minute," Elina said from behind me.

"Thanks."

"I don't understand."

"I very nearly didn't understand it, either," I said.

We sat on opposite ends of the sofa, leaving the entire middle cushion between us as if by mutual agreement.

"You're not yourself."

I didn't say anything. I was still gathering my thoughts.

"Tapani," Elina said quietly, leaning toward me. "You must have misunderstood what I said. About what happened. About Pasi Tarkiainen."

"I think I understood you perfectly."

She hesitated.

"I hope you won't tell Ahti everything."

I looked at her, wanting to say that I would hardly need to, when Ahti came into the room.

"Tapani. Hi."

He looked like he had lost several kilos in the past twenty-four hours, like he had got shorter, or somehow lost something of his outer form. I knew that it wasn't possible, but that was the impression I had as I looked at him in his sweatpants and wool sweater, with thick white athletic socks on his feet. He looked around and decided to head toward the armchair. Elina withdrew farther into the sofa, and away from me. Ahti sat down on the chair and looked at me.

"Elina said there was something you wanted to talk to me about."

I glanced at Elina, then at Ahti.

"I didn't say there was something I wanted to talk to you about. I just asked her to wake you up."

Ahti folded his hands in his lap and leaned his head against the back of the chair. He may have been trying to look the part of the lawyer more than the situation or his attire would allow.

"You don't sound like yourself," he said.

"How do I usually sound?" I asked. "Like a friend? Like someone who doesn't notice anything? Who believes everything I'm told?"

Ahti glanced quickly at Elina.

"These are tough times for both of us. I was bitten by a rat, which wouldn't be any big deal, but it completely changes our plans. I'm sure Elina told you that we're staying in Helsinki."

"Yes, she did."

"I had a high fever last night, and I'm still a little under the weather. And really tired. If there's anything we can do for you and Johanna, we'll do it. But it's no help to any of us if you come here behaving badly and bullying Elina. Our friendship doesn't give you that right. Especially in times like these."

I looked at Elina again. She was now sitting as far from me as the sofa allowed. She lifted her foot onto the seat and wrapped an arm around her leg.

"I wasn't trying to bully Elina," I said. "But if I did so inadvertently, I'm sorry. As far as what friendship means in times like these, I completely agree. It's everything else that has me a bit amazed."

Ahti crossed one leg over the other, leaned slightly to the left, put his elbow on the armrest, and lifted his chin. In other circumstances his posture would have radiated expertise and secure superiority. But clothes make the man, especially if he's a lawyer. Sweat pants and cotton socks will undo just about anyone's attempt at dignity.

"When Johanna disappeared," I said, and looked at my watch, "about forty-eight hours ago, I was in a panic, just as any husband would be. And since I don't have any family, I turned to my friends. I came here. You were leaving. At that very moment. That's a hell of a coincidence. And when I told you why I'd come, you immediately agreed to sell me a gun. Normally you're an absolute stickler about everything—especially anything to do with the law or with guns. But I didn't even think twice about it. I didn't stop to wonder why our closest friends hadn't told us they were leaving town."

When neither one of them seemed to want to say anything, I continued.

"I didn't even suspect anything when you told me that you hadn't been able to sell the apartment, because the place had so much wrong with it and the building was in such bad shape, with water in the basement and holes in the roof.

Then it occurred to me to check the facts. This apartment was never for sale. No one has tried to sell it to anybody. As far as the rest of the building: An apartment upstairs was just sold. Two floors up. Two floors closer to the holes in the roof."

I felt a strange burning in my throat, rough and distracting. It made it hard to swallow, and it was difficult to ignore. Shadows flashed at the edge of my vision: the physical symptoms of fatigue and betrayal.

"Then it started to bug me," I said once I got my throat cleared a bit. "I started thinking, Why do they want to leave Helsinki, if they can't sell their apartment? Why be in such a hurry to leave right now, when Elina's best friend is missing?"

Ahti laid his hand on the arm of the chair and wrapped his fingers over the end of it. It looked like he was holding the chair down, or holding on for the ride.

"Tapani, I've been very ill. This sort of thing doesn't exactly perk me up."

I paid no attention to his comment. I had to keep going.

"I thought, I have to ask Ahti about this. I'm sure there's a perfectly good explanation for everything. I can trust Ahti. He's a good friend, an old friend. But how good a friend? I was starting to wonder."

Ahti shook his head.

"Tapani, you're upset about Johanna's disappearance. We completely understand."

"I started thinking," I continued, paying no attention to him. "Why did Ahti say that he hadn't worked in two years, when I was easily able to find out that his last case was just last week?"

Ahti rubbed his forehead as if overcome by a sudden headache.

"You were one of the attorneys for A-Secure," I said, "when they started to expand. They're a pack of thieves, Ahti. They use violence. They rob people, beat people up, they may even kill people. But you work for them anyway."

We were silent for a moment. I wondered where I was headed next. Ahti looked at Elina, and I saw a little smile on Elina's face out of the corner of my eye—not a smile of amusement, but of love, attachment. She nodded. He nodded back.

"All right," he said, or rather whispered, looking at me. "I don't know if you've ever noticed, Tapani, but I've always been pretty quiet about the details of my work. I've had my reasons. And I've also had my reasons for working for the company you mentioned."

I tried not to get worked up. I spoke as precisely and calmly as I could: "Johanna figured it out somehow. She found out that you had been working for companies like A-Secure for years. She got in touch with you about it. I found out a few hours ago when I read her e-mails. She got in touch with you, and then something happened. Something happened to Johanna, and to you. What happened that made you have to pack your bags and leave all of a sudden?"

Ahti was just about to open his mouth when Elina said, "We're still your friends."

I gave her a sideways glance. She continued: "What happened had nothing to do with whether we're your friends or not. Johanna's my best friend. We didn't know everything would go to hell like this."

"When you work for criminals, things have a habit of going to hell," I said.

"Not like this," Ahti said.

I stared at him. He stared back.

"For the last time," I said. "What happened?"

They went through their nodding ritual again.

"Johanna called me," Ahti said. "She told me about those murders—when and where they happened. Then she told me her theory, which seemed unbelievable to me at first. But I had been handling A-Secure contracts by the hundreds, and I remembered quite clearly where they had contracts with companies, and directly with tenants and homeowners' associations. I didn't need to go through very many files to realize that the murders were in the same areas, even the same homeowners' associations. Then I looked at A-Secure's contact registry to check the dates of the initial contacts and the final agreements."

He shook his head and rubbed his forehead again, harder this time.

"It went neighborhood by neighborhood: First they sent a salesman through an area of the city, then the murders happened, and immediately after that, they would get a heap of contracts for surveillance, security guards, alarm systems, all kinds of services. They made a big pile of money very fast. Johanna figured it out."

Ahti raised his eyes.

"I didn't know what to do, who to tell about it, or what to tell them."

"The police didn't occur to you?"

He shook his head again.

"How would they have been able to protect us? How quickly could they investigate anything or link anything to A-Secure? And there was no way I was going to testify. I knew where it was in the company that these things were happening, and I had a good idea why."

"Who did you tell about it?" I asked.

"Elina."

"Nobody at A-Secure?"

He sighed.

"There's one other thing."

"What?" I asked.

"The contracts I was talking about, the ones that were signed right after each murder, were all written by the same person. The reason I wanted to get to Norway is because the person who wrote them was the head of the company himself. I've only seen him a couple of times in passing. You see, A-Secure is really just two men and a very effective ad campaign. Everything else is subcontracted."

I had an idea that seemed like a long shot but worth a try. I asked, "When was A-Secure established?"

"About four and a half years ago," Ahti said.

"Who set it up?"

"Harry Rosendahl and Max Väntinen."

I dug my phone out of my pocket, found the picture I was looking for, and turned the display toward Ahti. He squinted, got up from his chair, took the phone in his hand, looked at the photo for a moment, and said, "He's a lot younger here, but that's him. Harry Rosendahl."

He handed the phone back to me.

Pasi Tarkiainen still looked out at me with that infectious smile that always seemed to demand an answer.

23

THE DUSK OF A SOFT JULY EVENING CREEPS INTO THE APARTMENT. The objects in the room and their shadows merge with the summer air, the soft sofa is bottomless in the darkening room. I hear Johanna's steps on the wood floor of the kitchen, chopping fresh ginger for her tea, stirring it, adding something—honey perhaps—stirring it again. I can hear the delicate clink of the spoon on the thin lip of the wide-mouthed cup. I can almost even hear the cup lifted from the table, although that couldn't actually make a sound.

Then Johanna is in the room sitting beside me, and I can smell her hair and the green tea flavored with fragrant ginger and dried orange peel.

"I could make some for you, too," Johanna says, her voice as soft as the darkening evening.

"No, thanks," I say.

She tastes her tea, sipping it carefully from her spoon. The cup steams in front of her face.

"So it's just the two of us," she says after a moment.

I wrap my arm around her.

"No parents," she says. "No children."

I look into her eyes. There's not a trace of sadness in them. If anything, there's belief in life, courage. She scoops up her tea one small spoonful at a time, her lips puckering as she empties each one.

"Did you watch the news?" she asks.

"Yes."

"We've been there before. It was our first trip together."

"It's gone now."

"A lot of things are gone."

"That's what I was thinking," I say. "That there are so many things that are gone now."

"That's like fretting over the length of a meter."

"No, it's not."

"Yes, it is." She smiles, looking intently at her cup of tea, as if something had disappeared into it. "A meter's a meter. There's nothing you or anyone else can do about it."

I laugh.

"All right," I say. "A meter's a meter. The earth is burning up. There's nothing to be done."

Johanna looks at me, not smiling anymore.

"And it's just the two of us. What do you think about that?"

"I think about you," I say. "I think, I'm with you."

"Is that enough?" she asks, not looking at me.

"It's enough," I say. "But that's the wrong way to put it. I'm happy with you. That's what I wanted to say."

She tastes the tea from her cup, her upper lip reaching half a centimeter over the rim. She slurps the hot tea into her mouth and swallows carefully, concentrating. We sit in silence.

"What do you think about all this news?" she asks.

"I'm not surprised," I say. "It's not like there haven't been signs it was coming for a long time."

A few motes of dust dance in the last rays of sunlight.

"How long have we been together?" she asks, her smile not far off.

"Don't you know?"

She laughs.

"Silly," she says. "I'm asking if you know."

"Of course I do."

"Six and a half years."

"I'm surprised. You remembered."

"Of course I remember."

She drinks her tea. It's cooled a little, and she sips it normally now.

"The best years of my life," I say.

"These years?"

"Yes," I answer. "The last six and a half years."

"Same here."

She chases the bits of ginger in her cup with her spoon, they try to escape, and she quickly outflanks them. Finally gathering a sufficient quantity of ginger, she laps it up. I listen as she chews the raw ginger in her mouth. I love this woman so much—her personal, peculiar, even kooky habits.

"What would you change if you could?" she asks, once she's eaten up her ginger and taken a gulp of tea.

"I don't know," I say. "I read a book once where anytime someone changed one little thing everything, the whole world, would change. And that may be true. In fact, I think it is true. If I were to change something, it might accidentally have an effect on everything else, might change things that I don't want to change. I don't want to change this."

I give Johanna's shoulder a squeeze. She's wiry. The muscle under her shirt is a small, tight ball. She works out, and you can feel it when you touch her.

"You wouldn't even change this day?" she asks.

"Not even this day."

She puts her cup down on the coffee table, and the shadows take hold of it, its outlines softening, its contents invisible, completely dark.

"I could be wrong," Johanna says.

"About what?"

"I used to think that if I got news like we got today the whole world would fall apart."

"It's not going to fall apart."

"No, it's not," she says.

We sit in silence. Somewhere in the distance a door opens and closes. A brief blast and an echo, then it's perfectly quiet again.

"What now?" Johanna asks.

"What do you mean?"

"From now on?" she says. "What's next?"

"Nothing in particular, I guess," I say. "The world keeps on turning. We love each other."

"And then?"

"Like I said. The world keeps on turning. We love each other."

She laughs.

"You're quite a one-track guy."

"You married me."

"Yes, I did. And I was wrong."

"How so?"

"I was wrong when I thought I needed something else to be happy."

"What do you need?"

She walks two fingers up my arm. It feels pleasant, but it tickles a little. The dust motes' dance has gone wild—a draft of air is moving across the room. It must have come from the open window in the kitchen.

"What do you need to be happy?" I ask again.

"This. You. Us."

We sit in silence.

"Did you write today?" she asks.

"Every day," I say. "That's how I know where I'm going."

"Anything good? In what you wrote?"

"Maybe."

"You don't know?"

"Sometimes you know right off, sometimes not till later."

"What about now?"

"A little later," I say, "or maybe a lot later."

Johanna turns toward me. She picks up her legs and lays them across my lap. Her feet are bare and her toes are almost cold, although it's been one of the sunniest of summer days. I rub the soles of her feet and fold her toes in my hand. The little bundle of toes fits in my fist.

"I don't want to say this," she says after a moment.

"Don't say it."

"It's already on its way."

"I guess you have to, then."

She waits a moment.

"What if something happens to one of us?"

"Something bad?" I ask. "Or something irrevocable?"

"Is there a difference?"

"There's a big difference."

"What if one of us dies?"

"The other one will still be alive."

"No, really."

From the open kitchen window you can hear someone ride their bicycle into the yard and put it on the bike rack. Then they lock the bike. The door of the building opens and closes.

"Life goes on," I say.

"You always say life goes on."

"Because it always does."

"Except when it doesn't."

"I don't know," I say. "Everything in its time, I guess."

"If something happens to me," she says, "I hope it doesn't get you stuck. I hope that your life will go on."

"Likewise," I say.

The dust motes have less sunlight shining on their dance.

"But then," she says, "if something happens to me and your life goes on in the wrong direction, I'll definitely come and say something about it."

"I knew there was a catch."

"Naturally," Johanna says. "There's a catch."

I rub her feet and watch her close her eyes. The soft, safe darkness surrounds us, and Johanna's lips curl into a little smile. She's about to fall asleep, or about to laugh.

24

"You've got to understand," Elina said, but there was no conviction in her words. She didn't believe them herself.

Friendship doesn't end with a bang but with a flop, a letdown. I noticed Ahti wasn't saying anything. I walked to the front door and pulled on my coat and shoes. For some reason, I turned around in the doorway. Ahti and Elina were standing at the other end of the entryway. They might as well have been standing in outer space.

What was there to say? Let's treasure the memories of the good times, all the fun we had together? Let's not let a small thing ruin a big thing, something that was complete and beautiful at one time? I went through the alternatives. I couldn't think of anything better than "Good-bye."

They say that if you don't learn anything else in your life, at least learn to walk slow. I walked, deep in my thoughts, to the intersection that I'd been looking at on the surveillance video, without seeing anything.

The sun had set a while earlier and the sky was completely

dark. The rain that had no beginning or end had lost its passion and power for a moment. The sky trickled little drops of rain here and there as if it had decided to scatter them, sow the earth with them, but then changed its mind and preferred to save its seed. I couldn't be bothered with the cars honking their horns or the shoving pedestrians as I made my way down the street.

There was an acrid smell of burning plastic coming from somewhere, but I didn't look around to see from where. The smell followed me for several minutes. I wiped the drops of rain from my face and realized I'd left my gloves somewhere. A disco across the street had its door open, and a steady, loud, menacing beat pulled people in. I looked at my watch, then looked at my phone. Time was passing. Johanna hadn't called.

The last couple of days had been like one entire lifetime: voracious, crammed full, desperate. The buses and cars sped past with their motors yelling, and the exhaust left a dryness in my throat that I couldn't swallow. I could taste gasoline and exhaust on the roof of my mouth, nauseating and provoking me. A group of youths came rushing toward me and I tried to move to avoid them but failed. I didn't know what language they were yelling or why they were running. Two security guards ran after them. I understood their language. The young people kept running, although the guards shouted at them in Finnish to stop.

I reached the intersection, saw the camera bolted to the wall about ten meters up, and felt the raindrops falling on my eyelids. I looked in the direction the camera was pointed. I could see the intersection—both Urho Kekkosen katu and Fredrikinkatu. Hundreds of people, traffic, lights. All the things I'd been searching through trying to find Johanna.

Sometimes you don't find something until you stop looking for it. That's what Jaatinen had said.

I called him.

I COULDN'T BE SURE, of course, but I thought that the seven people sitting at the computer terminals were the same ones I'd seen there before. The focused, worried looks seemed to have frozen on their faces. I heard the clicking of keyboards under strong fingers and was sure that questioning gazes were following us, but when I looked quickly behind me I saw that no one had taken the slightest notice of us.

We were in the same workroom as before. I opened up the database with my password. We had exchanged only a few words on the way from the lobby to the second floor. Jaatinen seemed to be not just as weary as usual but also vexed, distant, like he wished he were someplace else, and even if he were he'd be just as cranky. This was a new side of him.

Jaatinen sat up straight in front of the terminal and looked at me, about to say something. I could see from the look on his face that his mind really was elsewhere. Whatever it was he wanted to say, he was taking a long time with it. Then he used a hand to help him. He pointed to the screen and promised to come back in half an hour to see how I was doing. I told him I didn't think it would take half an hour.

He looked at me again, as if I weren't really there. Then he turned and walked out of the room without saying a word. His steps were hurried, indignant. He disappeared into the stairwell, leaving behind a scattered, irritated feeling that threatened to take hold of me, as well. I got to work.

There were a confusing number of surveillance cameras. Although some of them were dark, enough of them were working to form a clear visual record of almost the entire downtown area. A few streets and intersections could be examined from multiple angles and several different elevations.

I went back to the time and the place where I'd already spent many hours: the corner of Fredrikinkatu and Urho Kekkosen katu, the geographic point where Johanna's phone had last been connected. The picture was just as rainy and glistening wet as I remembered. I let the stream of images flow by.

As the video approached the moment when Johanna's phone was turned off, I leaned forward instinctively. The picture was as confused and full of reflections as before, more like a painting than a photograph or film. Almost exactly one minute before zero hour I saw someone at the other end of Urho Kekkosen katu that I seemed to recognize before I possibly could have. But then, Johanna's e-mails had told me who to look for.

At that point the figure was still little more than two perfectly executed brushstrokes, their movements indicating haste. The figure took long, strong steps, coming closer second by second, growing first from two brushstrokes into many, then into a human form with distinguishable, individual features: the way of walking, of looking to the side, of shoving a hand in a pocket. I watched a moment longer to be sure I was right.

The figure reached the street corner, took something out of a pocket, touched it with one hand, and put it away again. At that exact second Johanna's phone was disconnected from the network. A large truck crossed the intersection, followed by an emergency vehicle with its lights flashing. The picture was like an impressionist painting again for a moment, and I realized how little I had understood when I watched it before. When the truck and the ambulance had passed, the figure stood at the crosswalk for a moment, so motionless that I wouldn't have known it was a person.

I paused the video and enlarged it. The figure grew and became more recognizable little by little. When all that would fit on the screen was the face, I adjusted the brightness and leaned back in my chair. Gromov, right down to the stubble on his chin.

25

FROM: Gromov, Vasili
TO: Lehtinen, Johanna
SENT: Dec. 21, 01:37
SUBJECT: One last favor

Johanna,

I want to make it clear one last time that I know where you stand. I understand when you say that you're happily married and we're just colleagues. And I understand why you don't want to work with me anymore after this assignment, even if it does seem very sad and unfair. I sincerely want to honor your decision to work with some other photographer going forward. But I have one small favor to ask before you do. Before our roads diverge, I want you to think about it one more time and remember all the things we've been through together. Remember in Kosovo, when we came under fire? Remember whose shoulder you clung to, who it was that protected you? Remember when our bus died at the edge of the Arctic Sea and the cold wind threatened to freeze the lot of us? Remember what you said when I got the motor running again? I remember. You said you would be forever grateful to me. Forever, Johanna. Those were your words. Now I'm asking you for a favor. If you really meant what you said, you'll grant it. You'll agree to it in order to be true to yourself as well as to me. You'll agree to talk about this face-to-face, and you'll speak the truth. I think it's the least you can do for someone who saved your life. And if, after we've talked, you still believe that I don't belong in your life, I'll accept it. But I'm asking you for one more chance, one more chance to talk to you face-to-face. I'm afraid that if you don't, I'll have to approach you again through a third party.

Vasili

26

I FOUND THE ROW HOUSE IN MAUNULA, NEXT TO KESKUSPUISTO, AT the north end of the park. The building was faced in red brick, built in the 1950s, and contained six townhouses. Judging by the lights in the street-side windows, all the apartments were occupied. Gromov's apartment was next to last on the right. A pale light glowed from the upstairs window.

It had been easy to find his address, of course, but getting Jaatinen interested in it proved impossible. When I had showed him the e-mail messages and the surveillance images all he did was concur that I might have something there. I lost patience with him. I might have something? And when I asked him to come with me, he said he didn't have time. That ended our conversation.

I asked Hamid to stop the cab and turn off the motor in front of the small, parklike area across from the building. The trees, bushes, and darkened lampposts offered some cover, which seemed sufficient for the present. I didn't intend to ring the doorbell. I also didn't want to make the same mistake I'd made in Jätkäsaari—I still had the pain and the bruises to remind me. It seemed wisest to first survey the situation, then start my approach on foot. I waited a moment in the dark, listening to the rain falling softly on the trees and bushes, the soothing drum of the drops on the dead wet leaves.

The building was separated from the house on its left by about ten meters. To the right stood a broad, dark swath of woods; the next nearest row house lay about seventy meters beyond it. The light from its nearest windows sparkled between the tree limbs in runaway rays.

I crossed the street to a trail that led through the woods. The sodden sand of the path made sometimes grinding, sometimes squishing noises underfoot no matter how hard I tried to walk lightly. The trail was drier, and quieter, at the edges. A little farther on I found an uphill path curving off toward the building. It had been trampled down to the roots of the trees by decades of use, and I had to be careful of my footing in the darkness.

The backyard wasn't fenced. There was a lawn that began at the back of the building and stretched to the edge of the woods. I looked in the windows a moment, didn't see any movement, and crossed the fifteen meters of grass to the back door. It wasn't until I was cutting across the small stone patio at the rear entrance that I noticed that one of the double doors, the one with the lock, was half a centimeter ajar.

I stopped to listen. The rain tapped against the windowpanes, pounded the surface of the patio table, and filled the woods with a murmuring sound. A car accelerated somewhere, slowed, accelerated again. There were no human sounds. The air had that slightly sour smell again, like the earth was already too wet, soaked through many times over, worn out.

I opened the door without a sound and entered a small

room with a fireplace, decorated with opulent good taste. A staircase at the back of the room led up to street level. I climbed the stairs to the living room, which was joined to a kitchen and dining area on the street side of the house. Light spilled in through the windows from the illuminated porch, drawing long shadows on the floor and creating dark hiding places along the walls. I stopped and listened. The only sound was my heartbeat. It seemed to echo off the walls, which were covered in framed photographs. There was a staircase in a cage of airy latticework in the middle of the open room, and the light that I had seen from the street seemed to be glimmering from the top of the stairs.

I went up the stairs one step at a time, saw a lamp on a night table softly illuminating a room, and then heard an anguished, choking voice ahead of me to the right.

"Who's there?"

I recognized Gromov's voice, although it was raw and hoarse, like he'd been struggling to breathe for a long time. I stepped into the room, and both of us were frightened, but I was the only one who recoiled. Gromov didn't move. He was lying on the bed fully dressed, his hands and arms stretched out, wet with blood. The bed around him was like a pool he was floating in. The room smelled of feces and something like raw meat.

"I can't feel my body," he said, struggling to speak.

I looked at him, bathed in blood. And I reminded myself why I was there.

"Where's Johanna?"

"I can't feel my body," he said again, as if he hadn't heard my question.

"Vasili, listen to me. Are you alone here? Has Johanna been here?"

Gromov let out a rasping sound that ended in a sputter that nearly choked him.

"Vasili," I said. "You have to help me. I'm looking for Johanna, and I know what story you were working on. I know about the Healer and about Pasi Tarkiainen."

I took a couple of steps closer and stood about where his waist was. There was a depression in his chest, darker than the blood. His face seemed surprisingly calm considering the fact that his chest was struggling and twitching with a life of its own. He seemed to be paralyzed. Perhaps the bullet that had ripped his chest open had also drilled a hole through his spine.

"I know about you, too," I said. "I have the message you sent to Johanna."

I was about to take my phone out of my pocket and show it to him, when he spoke.

"There's something else. Besides Tarkiainen."

I dropped the phone back into my pocket. Gromov's eyes had a searching look in them now. He said something, but I couldn't understand him. I leaned closer. After a moment, I understood. Love.

"I did it for love," he said.

"What?" I asked. "What did you do for love?"

He looked like he couldn't get enough air. He was clearly trying to express himself with minimal words.

"Johanna. I wanted her to understand that I still love her. Tarkiainen promised to help me."

"How could Tarkiainen help you?"

The question echoed through the room, hurried, impatient. The words sounded like they came from outside myself.

"Johanna wouldn't listen. I wanted another chance."

"A chance to do what?"

"I wanted her to realize that I love her."

Of course. And to show her that you love her, you deceived your longtime colleague and led her into the hands of a murderer.

"Tarkiainen promised," Gromov continued hoarsely, "that he could make Johanna understand my situation. And he had to meet with her because he had information about the Healer that he could tell her only in person."

Gromov's words came out half-whispered, half in a series of quick yelps, all of it running together.

"Tarkiainen knew so much," he said, sounding like he was running a foot race. "About Johanna, me, everything. I arranged to meet Johanna—told her I had a tip. Tarkiainen was supposed to talk to her and then bring her here. So we could talk in private."

He stopped speaking like he'd hit a wall and struggled to breathe. There didn't seem to be any more air going into his lungs than was coming out. He forced out a few more words: "But then Väntinen came here. And now look at me."

"Johanna's phone," I said. "You had it in your hand."

He tried to nod. His eyes closed and his chin jerked. Somehow, he got some oxygen.

"One more thing, to say," he said. "To you."

I looked into his eyes, where hope and hopelessness were taking turns. Like a man hanging on to a rope that can rescue him as time after time it slips out of his grasp. I waited as long as I could bear it. I was already turning away, looking for the phone, when he spoke again.

"You don't know how it feels," he said.

I didn't say anything.

"You don't know what love is. You don't know what it's like to lose the one you love," he said, "and then get her back again."

What was he talking about? I kept quiet and looked at his glistening face, drained of all color.

"I've known Johanna longer than you have. You don't know everything."

He looked like he would smile if he only could. I shoved my hands in my coat pockets, a strikingly nonchalant gesture considering that a dying man lay before me with a hole ripped in his chest.

"We were young lovers," he said, and if a man with his life about to leave him can sound triumphant and proud, Gromov did. "Twenty years ago. Until she left me. Over a misunderstanding. Then life threw us together again. I've always been a one-woman man."

I looked at the bloody figure on the bed and took my hands out of my pockets.

"According to Johanna, you were anything but a one-woman man," I said.

His sigh was like a hacksaw on metal.

"I wanted her to be jealous. To feel the same gnawing jealousy I felt."

I shook my head, trying not to lose my patience. He could breathe only a few moments longer. I could see the same rude superiority in his eyes that I'd seen in the past. I didn't understand where he got his energy.

"Then she would know how it feels," he said, in a voice that was so like his normal voice that I almost jumped.

"Where's Johanna's phone?" I said.

"Johanna still loves me. Do you know how I know?"

"Stop talking bullshit," I said, trying not to raise my voice. "I need that telephone."

He struggled to breathe again, gulping the air for a while with his eyes squeezed shut. Once he'd got some breath he opened them again, still looking defiant.

"I know one thing," he said.

I didn't reply.

"In her hour of need, she didn't want to call you."

I looked at him, wanting him to die, and wanting him to stay alive.

"You're lying," I said, wondering if he could hear the uncertainty in my voice.

"Why would I lie?" he said, looking as if it took all his strength to speak. "Look at me. I'm just telling you what happened."

"Johanna would have called me if she could."

"She had a chance to call you," he said. At that moment, his chest stopped twitching. He noticed it, too, and hurried to speak. He only managed a few words: "But she didn't call you."

A look of amazement suddenly covered his face, his mouth opening and closing. His head nearly lifted off the pillow, then fell again. His eyes were left staring at the ceiling.

The stuffy dampness, the raw, rotten smell spreading from Gromov's dead body, and my own oppressive, chest-tightening thoughts couldn't all fit in that small space. His last words echoed through the room clearer than they had come out of his mouth. Before I left the room I looked around, opening drawers and closets searching for the telephone, but didn't find it. As I walked out the door, I turned around. Gromov lay motionless in a dark puddle, like a big, broken doll. I didn't know what I should think. I turned out the light and went downstairs.

I walked once around the half-darkened, open-plan second floor before I remembered what Gromov had worn in the surveillance footage. There was a coat rack just inside the door, and Gromov's thigh-length, dark overcoat hung neatly from a hanger there. The coat looked empty, spent, the shoulders slumped loose. It felt wrong to rummage through its pockets. The left pocket was empty, but I found what I was looking for in the right one—Johanna's phone. I held it in my hand, waiting for it to tell me what had happened, what was true. I pressed the power button, but the phone was mute.

Then I heard the sound of a car on the street moving at high speed. It stopped suddenly. I just had time to look out the window before the motor was turned off. It was a black sports car, with no one in it but the driver. The driver's-side door opened and Max Väntinen stood on the street. I backed away from the window and quickly scanned my surroundings.

Väntinen opened the door with a key as I pressed myself into the space between the drapes that covered the window and a projection of the wall. Väntinen walked inside with quick, heavy steps, then stopped. I couldn't see him, but I could hear him and feel his presence. He was a few meters away, and for a moment I was sure I could hear his breathing, his heartbeat, practically even the movement of the blood through his veins.

After an unbearably long time, he climbed the steps to the third floor. I hoped that I hadn't left any drawers or closet doors open or left anything in the room that would tell him I was on the premises. But something happened, because Väntinen immediately came stomping down the stairs and out of the house. I heard the car speed away, and only some time later dared to move.

Adrenaline and fear made my hands tremble and my breath shake as I glanced toward the front door. Although I could see that Väntinen's car had left, I nevertheless decided to leave by the back door and go back to the taxi the way I had come.

I opened the door and listened for a moment to the murmur of the rain and the many sounds it made as it fell on the stones of the patio, the rain gutter above, and the shrubs beside me. The trees in the woods stood a few meters away as if observing a moment of silence. Gromov was dead. I had just been hiding a few meters from the murderer. And I hadn't even thought of the gun, still in my backpack in the taxi. But why would I have brought it with me? I just wanted to find Johanna. I heard the sound of Gromov's words again: what he'd said was possible, but it didn't ring true. Johanna's phone felt hot in my pants pocket, even with the battery dead. It would have the answer to Gromov's last words, at least—something in the call record, the messages, the memos, or the pictures would offer the key to Johanna's disappearance a few hours before. It would make things clear.

The path wound through the rain among the slippery tree roots. I stepped in a puddle at one point; at another my foot sank into a soup of mud. I was making my way along the edge of the trail when I heard a voice behind me.

"How did I guess?"

I turned and saw Väntinen step from behind a large, gnarled oak tree onto the path. In his hand was a large-caliber pistol. Probably the same pistol that had torn Gromov in two. And one like it had, of course, killed whole families.

His face was cold and ugly in the scant light. The hood of his raincoat was pulled over his head, and the edge of it cast a shadow over the top of his face to the bridge of his nose and cheekbones. I couldn't quite make out his eyes.

"How is it that a guy as curious as you is still alive?" he said.

"You really shouldn't kill me," I heard myself say. "It would be no use to either of you."

"Either of who?" he asked.

The cold rain pasted my hair to my forehead and tickled my scalp. The lights of the next row house twinkled through the branches farther off to the left. I looked as hard as I could at Väntinen, but I still couldn't see his eyes in the deep shadows. His question seemed sincere, though.

"The two of you," I said. "You and Tarkiainen."

He nodded quickly.

"Of course. He's in this, too. A little difference of vision. Pasi is so idealistic. Always changing the world. I, on the other hand, just got sick of being so damn broke."

Looking at the barrel of the gun, I couldn't help but think of Gromov. I had to ask: "Is Tarkiainen still alive?"

Väntinen's lips spread into a smile for a moment.

"You're more interested in how your wife is doing, aren't you?"

He was right.

"Where is Johanna?" I asked, and realized I was shivering. The rain, wind, and nearly freezing temperature had taken their toll.

"I don't think I'm gonna tell you."

The barrel of the gun rose a couple of centimeters.

"Let you die without knowing. Nosy creeps piss me off, as a general rule. You, for instance. Would you be in this situation if you hadn't come into my bar whining about your old lady?"

I had to stall for time.

"Tarkiainen," I said, grasping at something, anything. "Was he the one who started all this?"

Väntinen's lips smiled wider.

"OK," he said. His voice was casual, superior. "Let's stand in the rain and talk. How did it all start? Pasi wanted to make the world a better place, as usual. This climate change thing. He said that certain people had to be held ultimately responsible for what they'd done. I said, 'Why not?'"

His smile evaporated, and the barrel of the gun rose again.

"Pasi said he was ready to use serious methods. But that's

what everybody says until you actually use serious methods. Same thing with Pasi. First a hell of a lot of bluster, then whimpering when the shit hit the fan. I thought it was a simple matter. Kill a few assholes and collect some money. Nobody suffers. Pasi had a problem with it. He couldn't be the Healer after all. I had to take care of that damned song and dance, on top of everything else I have to do."

I tried to look around. Väntinen noticed.

"Do you want to hear this or do you want to try to escape? Makes no difference to me. I'm just standing here trying to decide whether to shoot you in the head, the neck, or the chest."

I continued to shiver and kept my eyes on his shadowed face. He was standing about four meters away. I couldn't hear anything but the rain. No cars, let alone people. Where were all those supposed dangerous inhabitants of the park when you needed them?

"I thought you'd be interested," Väntinen continued. "I'm getting to your wife—a real pain in the ass, if you don't mind my saying so. Do you want to hear it or don't you?"

I nodded, shaking. The cold had sunk right to my core, into my bones.

"That's what I thought," he said. "It was the last straw, the last misunderstanding in this whole damn mess. It wasn't all your wife's fault, even if she is a fucking nosy bitch. As you know."

He smiled and continued.

"Pasi had a dream. He wanted to get some journalist to understand what he was doing. To get favorable publicity, if you can believe that. He said that once people understood what we were doing and why, they would realize it was necessary."

He was almost laughing now, the gun barrel swinging a few centimeters back and forth.

"And this is the best part—they would join us. What do you think of that idea?"

I didn't say anything. Väntinen noticed I was shaking.

"You're trembling with excitement. I wasn't so enthusiastic. But that didn't stop me. We had a hell of a good business going."

"Tarkiainen was in on that, too," I said.

"He was sort of forced into it. He was skeptical about the security firm. Afraid people would find out it was a business scheme and turn against us. That's why we needed a journalist who could understand—somebody who could see the bigger picture and tell the good side of the story to a wider audience. So he decided on his ex-wife."

"They were never married," I said. "Where is Johanna?"

Väntinen gave a short, cold laugh.

"Don't you understand? I'm not going to tell you. You wanted to know how all this started. Now you know. I'm not going to tell you anything more."

We stood for a moment in silence. The rain drummed and danced on the trees and sodden ground. I could hear a stream off to my left. Somewhere far away, deep within the woods, was the shrill whine of a chainsaw or a moped—so far off that it wasn't any use to me. I had to keep the conversation going.

"Why?"

"Why what?"

"Why in general," I said, looking at the place where his eyes were and seeing nothing but black shadows. "Why won't you tell me where Johanna is? Why did you kill innocent people?"

He shrugged so nonchalantly that we might as well have been talking about what to have for lunch.

"The end is near," he said lightly. "What does it matter what we do? There are two alternatives: be a pitiful bastard working as a bartender, scraping by, working in a shit hole, more and more miserable all the time, right up to the end, or you can head north, live comfortably in your own house, in peace. And how many of us are truly innocent, anyway? That's where Pasi and I think along the same lines. We've all spent decades knowing what was coming, but nobody wanted to do anything that would make the slightest bit of difference."

"Some people tried," I said, and felt that even my lips were trembling. "A lot of people."

Väntinen sighed loudly. A little cloud of steam appeared in front of his face and was almost immediately swept to the ground by the raindrops.

"Yeah, yeah," he said, suddenly sounding exhausted. "It was what it was. But I have someplace I have to be."

He straightened his shooting arm. The hole at the end of the gun's barrel seemed to grow, and I thought, This is the last thing in the world I'll see—a little black eye that will wink once and end everything.

The shot deafened my ears and shook my body, and I was certain that even the trees were swaying. Väntinen's hood flew off the back of his head. His face was missing something. A forehead, I realized. The shot, which had come from somewhere to my right, had knocked it off. Väntinen fell forward. The browless head smacked into the wet sand face-first.

Hamid came out from behind a tree, picked his way around the limbs and roots, and stepped onto the path. He looked different. His eyes were grim, his short, curly hair shone like steel wool in the rain, and the electric tremor in the cheeks of his thin face showed more clearly than before. In his hand was the pistol I'd left in my backpack. I looked at it, then at Väntinen.

Väntinen's hand still held his gun, its barrel now full of sand and mud. On one side of his head I could see white bone, rinsed clean by the rain. I looked up at Hamid.

"I wasn't always a cabdriver," he said.

CHRISTMAS EVE

27

A FIERY RED CHRISTMAS STAR SHONE IN THE THIRD-FLOOR WINdow, exactly in the middle of the darkened apartment house. The building around it guarded it like a flame within. The hum of the car heater and the patter of the rain on the hood were the only sounds I heard, once my hearing returned.

Hamid sat in the driver's seat without speaking. He had accepted my thanks without speaking, as well. He kept his eyes aimed to the front and sat still, just being there, like he might do something completely unexpected at any moment. He had put the gun into the glove compartment. I thought about asking for it back, but there didn't seem to be any point, somehow. He was the one who knew how to use it, that was clear.

We'd found Väntinen's car after a brief search. There was a meter-high berm separating the parking area from the road. I checked again to make sure that Johanna's phone was charging and that Väntinen's keys were in my coat pocket, and got out of the car.

The wind had subsided, at least momentarily. The fresh

night air smelled clean and sharp. Väntinen's car gleamed like it had just been washed, the raindrops on its black body shining like pearls. I sat down in the driver's seat.

The car was as clean inside as out. I went through the door pockets and the storage case between the seats. I found a chamois, work gloves, and a few coins. The only thing in the glove compartment was the auto manual. The small, cramped backseat looked completely unused. Except for the driver's seat, the leg space was untouched and clean. I got out and moved the seats back to look under them. I didn't find anything, not even dust.

I walked around the car and opened the trunk. It was small and crammed full. In the middle was a large athletic bag with a long steel zipper. I opened it: a man's clothes, presumably Väntinen's. After a moment of random rummaging I noticed that there were summer and winter clothes in it. It was Christmas Eve. Väntinen had meant what he'd said about going north. If he had his bags already packed, he must have been planning to leave soon.

I searched two other bags and a small backpack and found more travel items: extra clothes, bath products, shaving gear, and finally Väntinen's passport. I took the bags out and looked under the mat. Just a spare tire and a jack.

I closed the trunk and the driver's door and locked the car. I walked toward Hamid. His face still stared straight ahead, like a wax mask behind the wet windshield, and I realized I might be able to find out Väntinen's destination if I went back to where we'd left him.

The body was lying on the trail in the position it had fallen. The gun had sunk into the sand. The rain had whitened the bones of his skull even more and had so wet his clothes through that they were becoming part of the mud on the ground beneath and around them. For the second time that evening I put my hand in a dead man's pocket. The difference was that this time the coat had someone in it. I found a telephone, and dried it on my shirt as I went back to the cab.

Hamid had turned the radio on, and the taxi was once again filled with the familiar, unknown language, pounding out a thousand words a minute to a hip-hop rhythm. Maybe Hamid was trying to get things back to normal. I couldn't actually see the look in his eyes, so it may have been something else. I didn't ask him yet where he'd learned to shoot so well—where he'd learned to kill people. Maybe he would tell me himself sometime. Maybe someday I wouldn't be so deathly tired, and I'd have the energy to think more about it.

Väntinen's phone wasn't password protected, and I went straight to his message files. I didn't need to search long before I found what I was looking for.

The train ticket was for one person, but it was clear from the message that there would be two other passengers in the group, and that they were leaving tonight.

The departure time was in forty-six minutes.

28

THE STATION PLAZA WAS BUZZING AND BATHED IN THE RAW, NAKED glare of floodlights. The light was so bright that it seemed to shine right through the people on its way to the ground. All around there were shouts, arguments, pleas, entreaties, and threats. Trains headed north every hour, but even that wasn't enough to lessen the flood of people. More and more people kept coming from the east, the south, and the west. The market on the plaza teemed with ticket scalpers and purchasers of valuables, hundreds of thieves and swindlers with hundreds of tricks and swindles, and, of course, ordinary people, each one more desperate than the next. Every other person walking by seemed to be a cop, a soldier, or a security guard.

The cries of children and the threats and demands of adults mixed into one big strain of panic. I ran with long, quick strides all the way to the station building, slowing only when I thought I'd come into the field of vision of the guards with their assault rifles. I got in line at the security checkpoint, tried not to think of the minutes lost, and looked around me.

I knew very well that the two other passengers mentioned

on Väntinen's ticket could be someone other than Tarkiainen and Johanna. I didn't see any familiar faces in the spectrum of races and nationalities. The only familiar thing was the fear and helplessness lurking in their eyes. It was clear to all of us that only a fraction of those departing would find any sort of tolerable work, housing, or even food in the north.

Jaatinen was waiting for me as arranged. His face wasn't quite as distracted and sour as it had been a few hours earlier, but he also hadn't regained the self-assurance that had sustained him when we first met. Now he was a man who was clearly missing something, and he knew that it showed.

"Track twenty-one," he said, before I had a chance to greet him.

I was about to continue straight to the platform when he grabbed me by the arm. His tight grip, just under my shoulder, brought me to a stop.

"Tapani," he said in a low voice. "If we do find Tarkiainen—"

"We will find him, if we get moving," I said, wrenching my arm loose.

He took a couple of quick steps and stopped in front of me, his eyes boring into me.

"If we do find Tarkiainen, I can't arrest him."

"Why not?" I asked.

"There's a problem with the DNA results. To be precise, the problem is that the results are gone."

I didn't say anything. I just darted around him and headed for the door. He followed me and kept talking, but I heard only a few fragments of what he was saying: the server, crashed, backup copies missing, catastrophe. Track 21 was far off ahead and to the left. There were nine minutes until departure.

I made my way half-running through the heavy-looking suitcases, the backpacks stuffed full, and the people carrying them, some hurrying, some stuck in one spot. The hall under the high roof of the station was so full of noise that I could no longer hear Jaatinen's footsteps, or my own, on the asphalt. I could smell food vendors and human desperation. It was Christmas Eve, but there was nothing there to indicate it.

I passed whole countries and continents, crossed languages and dialects. Helsinki had finally become an international city. But this wasn't how we had imagined it.

Track 21 was jammed with people and their things, of course. The train stood at the platform, stretching out of sight. Väntinen's seat was in car 18. I ran right to the edge of the platform, dodging the people waiting there. Jaatinen followed. We must have looked like two particularly inept tightrope artists as we tried to make our way along the narrow, empty edge as quickly as we could.

I tried to count the cars as I ran. The mass of people hid the sides of the train from view, and counting them while performing my high-wire act was difficult. When I got to what I thought was car 16, I pushed my way back through the wall of people. A large, black-bearded man shoved me out of his way as I tried to look at the car number. I dodged the dirt-encrusted giant and the clinging smell of his sweat and waited for him to move on.

Finally I saw the number. Fifteen.

I continued along the platform with my shoulder almost brushing the side of the train and heard the last announcement to board in Finnish, English, Russian, and some other language. It became harder to walk along the outer edge of the platform and I had to push through the crowd to continue forward. In return I got shouts and a few shoves. An older, coal-eyed woman with a scarf on her head gave me a painful jab in the leg with the long metal tip of her umbrella.

Car 18 was in front of me. I tried to see along its whole

length. Jaatinen came up behind me. Before I had a chance to say anything, I heard him yell something and rush ahead. For a large, heavyset man, he moved quickly.

My first glimpse of Tarkiainen's face was in profile. Maybe he sensed Jaatinen running toward him. Maybe the look on his face changed ever so slightly. In a fraction of a second he made his decision, turned, and took off at a run. I ran after both of them.

Jaatinen was about ten meters from Tarkiainen when a suitcase on the platform caught him in the legs. He let out a roar. His left knee was bent inward at a strange angle. He fell straight on his face with only his left hand to catch him. I could hear his wrist crack.

I reached him as he held his injured knee and rolled onto his back. His face was frozen in pain. He curled his broken hand and pulled it toward his chest, then pulled his gun from its holster with his good hand and gave it to me. I didn't say anything—I had no time to even think. I just took the gun and kept running.

Tarkiainen jumped down onto the rails. I followed. I dropped off the platform and felt lactic acid already stiffening my muscles. My landing wasn't a springy one, it was a thud and a stagger. But I kept my footing, heard the metallic voice announcing departing and arriving trains, and felt a tiny drop of rain on my skin. On the left I could see glass office buildings rising up, their black surfaces gleaming like water over ice.

Tarkiainen had a head start, and I gulped for breath as I tried to catch up. He was approaching the grassy cliffs and old villas that lined the tracks at Linnunlaulu. The gun weighed heavy in my hand. With each step it was harder to carry. I got my run into a rhythm, matching my steps to the ties between the rails. Tarkiainen's back loomed larger. The rain, the dark night, and the wan light of the rail yard made visibility hazy and blurred. The crossbeams of electrical poles floated above us like an unfinished roof.

The cold, wet air tore at my throat and chest. When we reached the bridge at Linnunlaulu, where the rail yard narrowed between the stone cliffs, my legs felt very heavy. A commuter train arriving at the station rattled and wobbled on its tracks as it passed on our right. The tracks on the left were empty.

As I passed the cut stone of the cliffs, I was only fifteen meters behind Tarkiainen. But my legs were like cement—I was slowing down. The pistol felt heavier and heavier in my right hand, and I made a decision. I released the safety, as Ahti had shown me, lifted my arm straight toward the sky, and pulled the trigger.

Tarkiainen jumped, lost his balance, and stumbled. He looked behind him. I couldn't speak, just aimed the gun at him. He stopped. I gasped for breath and concentrated on holding the pistol in front of me and holding myself upright. My lungs wanted me to bend over and rest my hands on my knees, or better yet fall to the ground and lie there on my back. For some reason, Tarkiainen wasn't nearly as winded.

"You must be Johanna's husband," he said, not seeming at all surprised.

I nodded. I let my breathing level out and held the gun straight in front of me, although it was so heavy that my arm felt like it was going numb. I took a few short steps toward him. Not that I necessarily wanted to be any closer, but because moving hurt less and kept my legs from stiffening better than standing in one place.

"What are you going to do?" he asked. "Shoot me?"

I used all my willpower to calm my panting for a moment.

"If I have to," I said, and greedily sucked in some air.

I was standing five or six meters away from him now.

Another commuter train was already passing us on the right. It shook the ground and made my legs tremble. I could feel the deepest tones of the slamming sounds it made in my breastbone.

"Listen to yourself," Tarkiainen said, and repeated my words. "'If I have to.'"

His face was wet and shining, but otherwise appeared just as it did in the photos—confident and muscular, even handsome. There was an intelligent look in his eyes; his gaze was level, and his hair was short and modishly gelled. And there was nothing in his midlength coat, oxford shirt, jeans, and sneakers that my sense of style could find fault with. As he stood there on the railroad tracks, he looked like he could be posing for a fashion shoot: one of those spreads where they put pretty people in gritty environments—abandoned factories, old tradesmen's shops, or, in this case, rail yards.

My breathing was leveling out, but my legs were twitching and the arm that held the gun had lost all feeling.

"You know what I'm looking for," I said.

Tarkiainen didn't say anything.

"Johanna," I said, wiping the sweat and rain from my eyes with my free hand.

Tarkiainen's expression remained unchanged.

"You seem to have already found Väntinen," he said. I noticed he was looking at the gun in my hand. I glanced at it, too.

It looked the same as the gun that I'd left in Väntinen's hand, the one lying in the dirt, sinking into the mud of Keskuspuisto.

I nodded and looked at Tarkiainen again.

"Hopefully he got what he deserved," Tarkiainen said.

I nodded.

"A savage. A sick shit," Tarkiainen said.

"Who?" I asked.

"Väntinen. As you know."

"And you're not?"

He shook his head.

"Even though you participated in murdering whole families?"

"Väntinen murdered them," he said. "And he enjoyed it. I didn't kill them. I just did what I had to."

"And what was that?"

"There's no need to pretend to be horrified or shocked," he said. "You can be your own smart self and tell me you understand." He paused a moment. "Because if you're half as sharp as Johanna says you are, you do understand. You know very well that my purpose wasn't to murder families. My purpose was to show that actions have consequences."

"Tell that to those little children."

"What are they going to miss?" he asked, and took a step sideways. I moved my hand, following him with the pistol. "Food running out, clean water running out, everything running out. They're going to miss being slowly smothered, and eventually suffocated. What is there going to be that they would have got any pleasure from? Cannibalism? Plague? Everyone at war with everyone else on one gigantic trash heap?"

"Maybe they should have been allowed to decide that for themselves," I said, moving the gun a little to the left again. Tarkiainen took a few small side steps toward the outermost rail. There was nowhere for him to run.

"That was the whole problem in the first place," Tarkiainen said. His face was tense now, excited. "That everyone got to choose. Endlessly, with no limits. That's why we're here today. The two of us. You and I."

Another commuter train clattered and rumbled past on

the right. Someone had to eventually notice two men standing on the tracks. Where were all the guards and soldiers and police I'd seen in the station?

I glanced behind me. The station shone all the way through the rain, but it was likely no one there could see us in the darkness, half hidden by the rocks.

"Where's Johanna?" I asked in frustration.

"What's the rush? Let's chat a little," Tarkiainen said. A smile rose to his face. "Or you could always shoot me. Is that your plan? Or are you going to hand me over to the police?"

I remembered what Jaatinen had told me. The evidence had disappeared. Tarkiainen couldn't be indicted, or even arrested. If I told him that, he would walk away triumphant. Then I would have no choice but to shoot him. I didn't think I had that in me. On the other hand, I had heard that there's something in all of us that's ready to do almost anything.

"What do you want to chat about?" I asked, to win myself a few more seconds.

"Don't you want to know what this is all about?"

"Väntinen told me. Greed. Business. Plus a taste for murder, I might add."

Tarkiainen shook his head, displeased.

"None of those things," he said decisively, as if we were on a talk show rather than standing on railroad tracks with a gun between us. "It's about humanity, about what, in the end, is the right thing to do. Who do you think those murdered people were? Benefactors? Humanists? They were selfish, indifferent narcissists. They were the real murderers."

A short, dry laugh erupted from behind his tight smile.

"There's no other name for them. Even after they knew about the destruction they were causing, they kept doing it. They kept murdering—by lying. The worst thing is the deceit.

All that talk about being friends of the environment, about ecology, respecting nature. As if electronics wrapped in plastic or cotton irrigated with drinking water could ever be anything but a detriment, the cause of the destruction, replacing something irreplaceable with a pile of trash."

He took another step toward the outer rails. I followed him, stepping over one tie, then another. He continued talking, his voice rising: "You're an intelligent guy. You don't really believe that eating organic food or driving a hybrid car could solve the problem, do you? Or buying environmentally friendly products? What does that even mean? Why do marketers use Soviet-style language? That's like talking about liberation through communism. Do you understand, Tapani? We've been living in a dictatorship. Shouldn't dictators be opposed?"

He was standing next to the outermost track now. I had been listening and watching him without speaking. The ground started to tremble, and I glanced behind me. Another train had left the station. It would reach us within a minute.

"We're in free fall, Tapani. All we can do now is what our heart tells us is right. Defend what is good, even if we know it's too late."

The train shook the earth. I could hear steel against steel, the wheels screeching against the tracks.

"I'm on the side of good, Tapani. There was a time when I strove for nothing less than saving the world. Now that the world can't be saved, I have to make sure that good continues to live for as long as evil and selfishness does. Maybe justice isn't winning, but it's not completely gone."

The train let out a long, low warning sound. I lifted the gun, not knowing why. The train was almost upon us. I took a couple of steps backward and looked in Tarkiainen's direction again. He was standing in front of the train, in the middle of the tracks, lit up by its headlight. The low warning blast echoed from the rocks. Then the train passed just two meters from me and I couldn't see him anymore. I lowered my gun.

When the train and all its cars had roared past and its noise had faded, I looked warily across the rail yard. I directed my gaze to where I had last seen Tarkiainen and prepared myself to see . . . what? Pieces of a person, the white bone, the varicolored internal organs?

I saw coarse gravel, railroad ties, and the rails, shining in the night. When I raised my eyes higher I saw a tall fence, and beyond that a taller wall of rock glistening with rain. I looked to the side at the retreating rear of the train, and then that, too, was gone. All that was left were the tracks, reaching into infinity.

I looked in the other direction and saw the rail yard, the tracks like a vast steel web, and the brightly lit station on the horizon, shining like the world's largest campfire, burning steadily even through the veil of rain. No trace of Pasi Tarkiainen.

I turned around several more times. All I got was freezing rain in my eyes. The cold took its numbing hold on my body again. Finally, I shoved the gun in my coat pocket and walked back toward the station.

Someone was jumping from the platform onto the tracks and coming toward me with quick steps, every third or fourth step ending in a treacherous stumble. I recognized the walk—eager, decisive. The grayish-blue coat, which was hanging slightly crooked, and the baggy black pants were familiar. There was something strange about the hands though, held straight out in front like that, not swinging from side to side for balance. When I could make out the hair and face, I was sure. The hair was dirty and tangled, the face pale and wet. From closer up, I could see a bloody scratch on the right cheek and a dark blotch on the chin. Lips dry and cracked. I could see the plastic tie around the wrists now and the feverish light of complete exhaustion—but also persistence and strength—in the eyes as they fastened on me again and again.

Johanna stumbled against me. I kissed her hair, held her head against my chest. She clung to my chest, my face, and finally my hands. I could see in her eyes that she'd been drugged, and it was hard for her to speak through her dry lips, stiff tongue, and hoarse throat. The words came out short and rough, and I couldn't understand her. It didn't matter. I held her in my arms and murmured soothing words in her ear. I told her I loved her a thousand times.

I could see Jaatinen behind her. He had climbed, or been lifted, onto a baggage cart and driven it to the end of the platform. Sitting there in the rain, he looked like a ship's captain on lookout. He spread his arms, and I knew he was asking about Tarkiainen. I shook my head.

His arms fell to his sides and he sat looking at me and Johanna. His expression may have been one of bafflement or disappointment. I couldn't worry about that. I closed my eyes to better feel what was in my arms.

I walked Johanna back to the station. Her steps were short and unsteady, but they were headed in the right direction.

THE MORNING OF GOOD FRIDAY

29

THE SLIGHTEST CREAKING OF THE HOUSE, SCRATCH OF BIRD'S FEET on the tin-covered windowsill, or strong wind in the crowns of the pine trees that bend over the bedroom window, and Johanna will flinch. But then she falls asleep again almost immediately.

It's a brightening spring morning at the end of April. The sun comes up early and shines buttercup yellow as soon as it rises, bright and strong.

I'm careful not to touch Johanna. The slightest touch can wake her. The blanket is wrapped around her like a bandage. Her cheek presses deep into the pillow, and I can hear a quiet, steady sniffling from her nose.

I get out of bed without making a sound, close the bedroom door behind me, and walk into the kitchen. I make coffee and stand in front of the window. The surface of the bay at Vanhakaupunki is dazzling blue and ragged from the wind. Here and there around the bay you can already see the various shades of the coming spring, from pale buds to the deepest green.

There's almost nothing to remind me of the past Christmas. Johanna recovered physically a long time ago, of course. She still has nightmares and a wariness—a feeling of fear in certain places and at certain times—that she finds hard to admit, even to herself.

I pour some coffee, sit down at the table, turn on my e-reader, and read the news. For some reason it doesn't depress me anymore, although it gets steadily worse as time goes by. When I saw Jaatinen yesterday, he said it was because I look at life the same way that he does now—realistically, without baseless expectations, without looking backward. He seemed to be saying that I'm living life one day at a time. I didn't contradict him.

The purpose of his visit was not just to check up on my attitude. He told me the investigation was complete—they had verified that Väntinen had killed dozens of people and that Gromov had conspired with him and blackmailed Lassi Uutela.

I tried to tell Jaatinen that I already knew all that, but he didn't seem to want to hear what I was saying. So I let him go through the whole thing one more time. We also went through those minutes in the rail yard, without learning anything new. When he finally left, he had the same disappointed look on his face that he'd had at Christmas.

I don't know why I'm turning all this over in my mind when my eye falls on the instant message icon, which I click without thinking. It's Good Friday, and I'm not expecting anyone to get in touch with me.

The subject alone says a lot: THE BATTLE FOR GOOD CONTINUES.

I read the message. It's well written, clearly argued, and completely unnerving.

I get up and walk to my office. I get out the backpack that

I shoved to the very back of the closet at Christmas. Inside, I find what I'm looking for.

Just as I'm opening the bedroom door, I remember the frantic thoughts I had when Johanna disappeared. I remember wondering which was worse, complete certainty that the worst has happened, or fear, building up moment by moment. A sudden collapse, or slow, crumbling disintegration.

Maybe I should be satisfied now that I know the answer.

Johanna's eyelids flutter, the spring sunshine is relentless. It pierces through the fabric of the blinds and soon conquers the entire room. Johanna doesn't waken as I lie down beside her. She presses her head deeper into her pillow.

I can't resist touching her fingers. As I brush them lightly, they withdraw a bit at first, but then they let me intertwine my own fingers with them. Something happens when I touch Johanna. Something in my heart stirs, something says this is right—this is good.

And it is good. I'm a part of her, and she's a part of me. We're as happy as two people can be in this world. Whatever happens, I will love Johanna.

I wait patiently, and when she wakes up, I tell her why I have a gun in my hand.

ABOUT THE AUTHOR

ANTTI TUOMAINEN (b. 1971) was an award-winning copywriter in the advertising industry before he made his literary debut in 2007 as a suspense author. In 2011 Tuomainen's third novel, *Parantaja* (*The Healer*), was awarded the Clue Award for "Best Finnish Crime Novel 2011" and is being translated into 23 languages.